I0666825

The Adventures of a Boy Reporter

Harry Steele Morrison

Contents

THE ADVENTURES OF A BOY REPORTER

BY

Harry Steele Morrison

THE ADVENTURES OF A BOY REPORTER.

CHAPTER I.

LIVING IN THE COUNTRY--LIFE AT SCHOOL--THE HUT CLUB IS FORMED--THE COMING OF THE CIRCUS.

"YES," said Mrs. Dunn to her neighbour, Mrs. Sullivan, "we are expecting great things of Archie, and yet we sometimes hardly know what to think of the boy. He has the most remarkable ideas of things, and there seems to be absolutely no limit to his ambition. He has long since determined that he will some day be President, and he expects to enter politics the day he is twenty-one."

"Is that so, indeed," said Mrs. Sullivan. "Well, we can never tell what is going to come of our boys. As I says to Dannie to-day, says I, 'Dannie, you must do your best to be somebody and make something of yourself, for you and Jack bees all that I has to depend upon now.' But Dannie pays no attention to my entreaties, and somehow it seems to me that since Mr. Sullivan died the boys are gettin' worse and worse. It's beyond me to control them, anyhow."

"Oh, take heart, Mrs. Sullivan," said Mrs. Dunn, "our boys will all turn out well in the end, and all we can do is to bring them up in the best way we know, and trust to them to take care of themselves after they leave home. Now Dannie is certainly an industrious lad. I hear him pounding nails all day long in the back yard, and he made a good job of shingling the woodshed the other day. He seems made to be a carpenter."

"Yes, I think so myself," said the Widow Sullivan. "The whole lot of them is out by the railroad now, building a hut. They've organised a 'Hut Club' to-day, and never a lick of work have I had out of them boys since mornin'. They've always got something going on, and when I want a bit of water from the well, or a little wood from the shed, they're never around."

"Yes, but boys will be boys, Mrs. Sullivan, and we'd better keep them contented at home as long as we can. They'll be leaving us soon enough. It seems that no boys are content to stay in town any longer; they're all anxious to be off to the city."

"That's true, that's true, Mrs. Dunn," said Mrs. Sullivan. "I must be going now. I'm much obliged for the rain-water, and whenever you want a bit of milk call over the fence, and I'll bring it to you with pleasure. It's a good neighbour you are, Mrs. Dunn."

And Mrs. Sullivan went slowly around the house and out at the front gate, while good Mrs. Dunn returned to her ironing, a few clothes having to be ready for Sunday.

While these mothers were discussing their boys, the youngsters themselves were busy behind the barn, building a hut down near the railway track. There were six of them altogether, the three extra ones, besides Archie Dunn and the Sullivan boys, having come from across the railway to play for the day. Two hours before they had solemnly organised themselves into the "Hut Club," each boy walking three times around the block blindfolded, and swearing upon his return to be true to all the rules and regulations of the organisation, which had been written with chalk on the side of the barn. The regulations were numerous, but the most important one was that no East Side boys were to be allowed within the club-room when it was built, and that the club's policy should be one of warfare against the East Siders on every occasion when they met. This fight against the East Side was, indeed, responsible for the organisation of the club. It was felt necessary to have some head to their forces, and some means of holding together. So the club was organised, and now the next thing on the programme was the erection of a hut to serve as a club-house. Archie Dunn, who had been elected president, volunteered to get three boards and a hammer if the other boys would each get two boards and some nails. This proposition was agreed to, and when the boys returned from their foraging expeditions it was found that there were more than enough boards to build the hut, so the work began at once. Holes were dug in the ground, and some posts planted as supports for the structure, and then the boards were hastily nailed together from post to post. In three hours the hut was practically completed, and it remained only to lay a floor until they could hold their first meeting in the new club-house. The floor itself was down by noon, and the club then served a memorable dinner to mark the completion of the structure.

A hole was dug in the ground outside the door, and a furnace made. A skillet was brought from Archie's house, together with some dishes and a coffee-pot, and Dan Sullivan brought some more dishes, and six eggs from his nests under the barn. The boys were obliged to make several trips to and from the houses, but finally nearly everything was ready, and the eggs were carefully cooked by Archie, who was really a good housekeeper, from long experience in the kitchen with his mother. Some potatoes were fried in the grease remaining in the skillet after the eggs were cooked, and then the feast began. The eggs may have been rather black with grease, and the potatoes were certainly not done, but the boys all pronounced it the finest meal of their lives, notwithstanding the bitter coffee, and the dirty bread, which had been allowed to fall into the gutter beside the railway track. They were eating in their own house, and they had cooked in the open air, "just like tramps," Harry Rafe said, and it was little wonder that they enjoyed the novel experience.

The only trouble came when the meal was finished. No one wanted to wash the dishes, and, finally, it was decided to return them to their respective kitchens just as they were, and to let them be washed with the rest of the dinner dishes at home. And this decision came near putting an end to Hut Club dinners, for both Mrs. Dunn and the Widow Sullivan were determined not to wash any more dirty dishes from the hut.

When the meal was over, the boys lounged about the hut, and Dan Sullivan brought a lot of things from his sister's playhouse with which to furnish it more suitably. Archie Dunn brought a lot of hay from the loft in his mother's barn, and when a piece of old carpet was spread upon it it made an acceptable couch. A piece of old carpet was laid in front of the hut, too, where the boys could sit and watch the trains switching back and forth on the railway, and the tramps who were heating coffee in cans over by the cattle-pen.

Finally, some cattle arrived in the pen to be loaded into cars for the city, and the boys had just decided to go and watch the men loading them, when an engine came up the side-track with the most beautiful car they had ever seen, behind it. The car was painted in all colours of the rainbow, and in giant letters was printed the magic name of "The World's Greatest Show."

The boys lost no time in getting down from the cattle-pen fence, and the car had barely stopped when they were aboard. "Hooray," shouted Charlie Huffman, "we'll all get jobs of passin' bills." And it was with this end in view that they sought the advertising manager in the car, who promised to give them all jobs when the circus came in two weeks. The boys deluged him with questions of every sort. "Will there be any elephants?" "Is there goin' to be a parade?" and "Will there be any trapeze performances?" The poor man was finally obliged to lock the door to keep them out, and the boys stood about the car until nearly six o'clock, admiring the paintings, and speculating as to whether they would be able to work their way into the circus or not, when it finally came. Their speculations were interrupted by the appearance on the scene of the Widow Sullivan with a good-sized maple switch, which she used to good effect in getting the two Sullivans and Archie Dunn home for supper. For Mrs. Dunn had given Mrs. Sullivan instructions before she started, so that when Archie complained that he had been whipped by "that woman next door," he received no sympathy whatever.

And when he went to bed at nine o'clock, he could hardly sleep for thinking of the wonderful things which had happened this day. The coming circus and the great Hut Club kept him awake until far after ten, so that he got up too late for Sunday school the next morning, and was punished accordingly.

The next week was a hard one at school, and the boys had but little time to devote to the club. But after four o'clock in the afternoon they sometimes got together and did various things which improved their club-house. Some very fair chairs were constructed from empty soap boxes, and various contrivances were put together to guard against the intrusion of any East Siders or tramps while they were away at school. There was no padlock used, and any one coming up to the hut would imagine it a simple thing to enter--until he tried. But the boys had fixed a secret cord which, when pulled, shifted the bar inside, and every boy was sworn not to betray the existence of the cord.

The day set for the circus came nearer and nearer, and the boys began to be anxious for fear the schools would not close, so that they could attend. But the superintendent finally announced that they would; so early on the eventful day the entire club was on the grounds, waiting to get some work to do. Archie Dunn got the first job, being selected to carry water for the elephant because he was stronger than any of the others. But the rest were given something to do, and when the day was over they had all seen the circus, and went to bed happy, to dream of the great trip to be taken by the Hut Club on the next Saturday.

CHAPTER II.

THE Hut Club went out on a picnic the next Saturday, and had a jolly time. They camped upon an island in the middle of a shallow stream, and while there made coffee and cooked their dinner, having brought most of the necessary apparatus from the Hut. They fished a little, and hunted for turtles in the water, and altogether had a good time, if nothing exciting did occur. It was after nine o'clock at night when they reached town again, footsore and weary, and Archie Dunn had hardly entered the house before he was on the dining-room lounge, half-asleep. His mother seemed to be out, and as he lay there he wondered how long it would be before she came back. Archie truly loved his mother, but of late he had often thought that he would like to leave home and go to the famous city, where he felt sure he could get something to do. But he disliked the idea of leaving his mother.

"I'm getting to be a big boy, now," he often said to himself, "and it's time that I began to look out for myself. I'm nearly seventeen, and I think I ought to be earning some money. This thing of belonging to Hut Clubs and spending my time in going to picnics and to circuses ought to stop. It's all right for boys, but I'm getting to be a man, now."

All these thoughts were flying through his mind when his mother came in. "Oh, Archie," she exclaimed, "I've been so worried about you. I've just been over to Mrs. Sullivan's to see if Dannie had come home, and whether he had seen you. Wherever have you been?"

"We didn't think it would take so long to walk home," said Archie, jumping up from the sofa, "but we were awfully tired, and we didn't come very fast. I'm so sorry you were worried.

"And I'm as hungry as a bear, mother. Can't you find me something to eat?"

"Yes, dear," said Mrs. Dunn, softly, "and when you've finished your supper I have something for you. I won't give it to you now for fear you won't be able to eat, but as soon as you have finished your meal, you shall have it."

So Archie was obliged to eat his baked beans and brown bread and drink his milk without knowing what was in store for him, and he hurried as fast as he could, so that he could learn. When he had finished he went into the sitting-room, and found his mother sitting with a letter spread open upon her lap. "Uncle Henry has written me asking if you cannot go with him to New York on Monday, for a couple of days. He is obliged to go down there on business, and says he will be glad to take you along and show you something of the wonderful city, for he knows you won't be any trouble to him. Now I hardly know what to say, Archie. If I can feel that you are behaving yourself properly, and are doing your best to be as little trouble as possible, I am willing that you shall go."

"Oh, mother," cried Archie, "I'll promise anything. Only let me go this once, and I'll promise to stay at home all the rest of the summer."

"All right, then," said Mrs. Dunn. "You shall go on the first train Monday morning, and Uncle Henry will join you at Heddens Corner. Run along to bed now."

Archie went up-stairs almost dumb with delight Was it really true that he was to see the great city at last? He had heard some of the boys at school telling what their fathers saw there, but he had never even hoped that he would see it for himself so soon. Of course he had determined to see it all some day, but that was to be far in the future. The lad could hardly sleep for the joy of it all, and when he did finally lose consciousness, it was only to dream of streets of gold, and great buildings reaching to the skies.

Sunday passed slowly by. At Sunday school, Archie told the boys that he was going to New York on the morrow, and from that moment he was the hero of the class. The boys looked at him with wondering admiration, and seemed scarcely able to realise that one of their number was to go so far from home. The city was in reality little more than a hundred miles, but to their boyish minds this distance seemed wonderfully great.

Early on Monday morning Archie was at the depot waiting for the train. His mother was there to see him off, and there were tears in her eyes at the thought of parting with her only child, if only for a day or two. And Archie was radiant with delight at the glorious prospect ahead of him. He walked nervously up and down the platform, and wished frequently that it were not so early in the morning, so that some of the boys might be there to see him off. Finally, the great hissing locomotive drew up, with its long train of coaches, and Archie was soon aboard, hurrying off to Heddens Corner and the city. In a few minutes Uncle Henry was with him, a tall, fine-looking man, with an air of business. Uncle Henry kept the general store at the Corner, and was an important person in the neighbourhood. He was of some importance in the city, too, for his name was known in politics, and his custom was always desired at the wholesale stores. So Archie was going to see the city under good auspices, if his uncle would only have time to take him about with him.

After a couple of hours, during which Archie kept his face glued to the window-pane, watching the flying landscape, the great train pulled through a long, dark tunnel, and finally entered an immense shed, covered with glass where it came to a final stop. Crowds left the coaches, and passed out of the station, where they were swallowed up in the great rush of traffic. Some drove away in cabs and carriages. Some entered the street-cars, and some went up a stairway and entered what seemed to Archie a railway train in the air.

Uncle Henry told Archie to follow him carefully, and they, too, were soon flying away from the neighbourhood of the terminal, past hotels, stores, and dwellings, until they finally left the trolley-car, and passed through a cross street into a long, quiet thoroughfare which looked old enough to have been there for a hundred years. The houses were built far back from the street, with pillars in front, and into one of these quaint old dwellings went Archie and his uncle.

"I always stop down-town," explained Uncle Henry, "because I am near to the great wholesale establishments. It is central to the retail stores, too, and to many of the places of interest."

When they were settled in their room, Uncle Henry explained that he would have to be away most of this first day, but that to-morrow he would take Archie out and show him the sights. So Archie expected to remain indoors all day; but when his uncle had left the house he decided that he couldn't possibly remain in this close room when so many wonderful things were taking place outside. So he decided to walk up and down the street, anyhow, and when he went out he felt like a prisoner just escaped from a cell. But the noise was terrible, and there were a great many wagons and trucks passing through the street. The greatest crowd seemed to be on that cross street about two blocks away, so Archie decided to go there, and see if there was anything new on that street.

He saw many wonderful things. There were cars running along without any apparent motive power, there were thousands and thousands of people in the streets, and the stores looked so handsome and interesting that he simply couldn't resist going into one or two of them, just to see what they were like. And when he had finished with one or two he could think of no reason why he shouldn't go on up the street, where he was sure he would find a great many more interesting things to see. So on and on he went, until at last he was tired and hungry, and then, for the first time, he was a little frightened, because he thought of all he had read about people losing their way in the city, and not being able to find their relatives again. But he was a brave boy, so he determined to make an effort to find his way back without appealing to a policeman. And after a time he was successful, and entered the queer old house in the ancient street at just three o'clock in the afternoon. His uncle was there waiting for him, and was nearly beside himself with apprehension.

"I was about to send out a general alarm for you, at the police station," he said. "How did you happen to go away?"

"Oh, I was so very tired of staying in the house," said Archie, "and I felt sure that I could find my way back without getting lost at all. And to-morrow I'm sure I can get along all right, Uncle Henry, so you needn't bother with me at all, unless you want to."

And it so happened that Mr. Kirk was very busy the next day, and would have found it quite impossible to show Archie about. So it was fortunate that he was able to go everywhere alone, or he would have had to return home without seeing anything at all of the city.

As it was, he went here, there, and everywhere, and saw a great deal of the city, the people, and the way in which they lived. The entire place had a strange fascination for him, and all the time he was thinking how glad he would be to live where he could see all this rush of business, this varied life, every day. And he fully determined to return some day and get something to do, so that he might work himself up, and come to own one of the handsome houses on the avenues, or drive one of the elegant carriages on the boulevard. And he observed every boy who passed him, and talked with several of them, trying to find out whether positions were easy to secure, and whether they paid much when they were secured.

So when they took the four o'clock train for home, and arrived at Archie's house in time for supper, he told more about the city boys and their work than about the tall buildings, the Brooklyn Bridge, or the Central Park. He talked so much, in fact, about the delights of the city boy, and the money he earned, that after he had gone to bed Mrs. Dunn took her brother aside and talked with him concerning Archie's future. And between them they definitely decided that Archie must not go to the city to work.

CHAPTER III.

ARCHIE DETERMINES TO GO TO THE CITY TO WORK--
LEAVING HOME AT NIGHT.

ARCHIE DUNN was not more ambitious than many other boys of his age, but he possessed one quality which is not developed in every boy, determination. Once Archie decided upon doing a thing, once he had made up his mind that it was truly a good thing to do, nothing could keep him from putting his plans into action, and making an effort, at least, to accomplish his ends. Most boys of seventeen have not decided what they want to become when they are men, and, until his visit to the city, Archie was equally at sea concerning his future. He knew, of course, that he wanted to be rich and famous, but when he tried to think up some suitable profession which would bring him these possessions, he was never able to decide.

The two days in the city with Uncle Henry had opened to his boyish mind a new world, and when he returned to the humble home surrounded by gardens, he felt that he would never be satisfied to live and work in this small town. There was now no question in his mind but what the city was the place for any one who wished to become either rich or famous. It would certainly be impossible for him to make a name for himself in this village, while in the city he would have every opportunity for improving himself, and advancing himself in every way. He wondered, indeed, that he had never thought of going to New York before, and was disgusted with himself when he thought of the time he had wasted here at home.

But there was no use in thinking of the past. The thing to do now was to get to the city as quickly as possible, for to Archie every day seemed precious, and each delay kept him further from the consummation of his hopes. It never occurred to the boy that his mother might have objections to his leaving home. She had always been very ambitious for his future, and he supposed that she would be delighted at the idea of having her boy in the great city, where he would have innumerable chances for improving himself. So when they sat on the front porch, one evening, and he told her of his plan, he was surprised to hear his mother pleading with him to remain at home. "Archie," she said, "I am almost sure you will come to some bad end in the city. You really must not go, for my sake, if for no other reason."

"But, mother, I can't remain here in town always. I must go out into the world some time to earn a living and make a place for myself, and I think the sooner I go the better, don't you?"

"Yes, Archie, but you're so young, and you've had no experience. You have no idea of the things there are in great cities to drag young men down. I don't think I could stand it to have you so far away from home and in such danger."

"Well, mother," said Archie, "there isn't much use in arguing about it. I have reached a point where I don't think I can be any longer satisfied at home. I have been here seventeen years, and I think I can remain here that much longer without improving myself. In the city I am sure I can make rapid progress, and in a year or two you can come there and live with me."

Archie got up from the porch and went down the street, while poor Mrs. Dunn ran over next door to see her neighbour, Mrs. Sullivan. When she had entered the disorderly kitchen, and seated herself on one of the home-made chairs, the anxious mother burst into tears. "I don't know what to think of Archie, Mrs. Sullivan," she said. "He is determined, now, to go to New York, and I know that if he goes I will never be able to see him again. I am nigh distracted with worrying over it. I have talked with him, but he seems determined, and I know I can never hold out against his entreaties and arguments."

"Sure, now, Mrs. Dunn," said the Widow Sullivan, "don't yez be a worryin' about 'im at all. That Archie is a smart boy, he is, and if he goes to New York he'll come out all right, never fear, I only wish my Dannie had as much get-up about him as your boy."

"Yes, yes, Archie is very ambitious for his age," said Mrs. Dunn, "but I some-times wish he were less so. I know I could keep him at home longer if he wasn't so anxious to be at work. I don't believe I can let him go, Mrs. Sullivan, not yet. I want him to stay in school another year, and then I'll think about it."

"Well, ye're wise, Mrs. Dunn, ye're a wise woman," said the Widow Sullivan. "Since yer husband died ye've been a good mother to the lad, and have brought 'im up well. And now, how is yer chickens, Mrs. Dunn? Have ye got that cochin hen a 'settin'' yit?"

And the two women began to discuss their various fowls, and the conversation was so interesting that Mrs. Dunn remained late, and found Archie in bed when she went home. "Ah, well, poor boy, I'll have to tell him of my decision in the morning. He'll be terribly disappointed, and I hate to do it I'm afraid it's selfishness that makes me want to keep him with me. I almost wish he would take things into his own hands, and start for the city himself. I would be rid then of the responsibility of sending him, and the question would be settled for me. Boys sometimes know best how to settle their own difficulties, anyhow."

Mrs. Dunn kneaded the bread before retiring, for to-morrow was Saturday, and, therefore, baking-day, and then she went into her little room off the kitchen, and prayed earnestly for her boy before sleeping. She prayed that she might be helped in advising him, and that he might always do what was best for himself and for his mother.

The next day was Saturday, and in the morning the Hut Club met, as usual, and prepared to have an open-air dinner for this day. The furnace, which had been knocked down during the week by the East Siders, was rebuilt, and the skillet and other utensils were brought from the nearest kitchens. Archie went to the grocery around the corner and bought five cents' worth of cakes, and then the six boys sat down in a circle and prepared to devour their home-made feast. But before they began Archie stood up. "I want to say that this will probably be my farewell dinner with the club," he said, in a low tone, "and I hope that you will appoint another president in my place."

The boys were horror-struck, but Archie refused to explain where and when he was going. Finally, they refused to appoint another president, all agreeing that Archie should hold that office for ever, wherever he was. And the meal was eaten in silence, for the announcement had thrown a sort of chill over the proceedings. When they had finished, Archie silently shook hands with each of the boys, who were dumb with amazement, gathered up his skillet and coffee-pot, and went home through the gate to the chicken-lot.

"I wonder what he's goin' to do," they all said, as in one breath, and as there was seldom much fun in the club when Archie was absent, they all went home in a few minutes, or down-town to watch the farmers, who were in town to do their weekly buying.

When Archie reached home he went up-stairs to his little room, and began to lay out a few things which he wanted to take with him, for he had determined to start for New York this very night. Then he tied the things up in a small bundle, and sat down to write a note to his mother. When he had finished it, he pinned it up at the head of his cot, and this is what it said:

"MY DARLING MOTHER:--Please don't worry about me, I'm bound to come through all right, and if anything happens to me, I promise   that I will write to you immediately and let you know. I have the   ten dollars which I have saved, and if I don't get work at once I   will write to you for some more. Now, I am not doing this thing for the sake of adventure, but because I am sure it is the best thing   for me, and I don't want you to worry at all. I shall write to you often and let you know just what I'm doing, so don't worry, but bea brave mother. I'm not going off this way as a sneak, but because I want to avoid a 'scene.'

"Your loving

"ARCHIE."

And at three o'clock the next morning Archie Dunn got out of bed, shouldered his bundle, and started off for the great city, which seemed to be drawing him like a magnet.

CHAPTER IV.

WORKING ON A FARM TO EARN SOME MONEY--CRUEL
TREATMENT.

WHEN daylight came, Archie was far out of the town walking quickly along the southern road. He figured that he had walked nearly six miles in the two hours since he had let himself out of the back door at home, and, as he looked ahead, he planned that he would walk at least thirty miles every day. Of course, he had never done much walking before, or he would have known better than to have expected to accomplish so much in twelve hours, but he felt fresh and full of strength this morning, and nothing seemed too hard to accomplish. As yet he had not regretted his departure from home. The excitement of it all, and the adventurous side of his exploit, had kept him interested, and made him feel that he was a real hero. But he was not so foolish as to imagine that there would not be times when he would regret having set out for New York. He was too old and too sensible for his age to allow his ambition to run away with him entirely, and he fully expected to meet with many great discouragements. "But I'm sure of one thing," he said to himself, as he walked along, "I never will return home until I have something to show for the trip. I won't have the club boys and the neighbours saying that Archie Dunn had to come home discouraged. If I return without accomplishing anything, I will be held up to the whole town as a boy who made a fool of himself by not taking his friends' advice, and I never will be made an example of if I can help it." And Archie walked faster as he thought of the possibility of failure.

When seven o'clock came he was passing through the county-seat, but though there were many interesting things to look at in the town, Archie determined not to stop. He was afraid he might meet some one he knew, who would be sure to ask him where he was going with his bundle, and what he was doing out so early. And anyhow he was very hungry, and decided to get out of the town and to the farmhouses as soon as possible. "I can work for my meal at a farmhouse," he said to himself, "but in the town they'll take me for a regular tramp."

So poor Archie walked quickly through the town, still keeping to the southern road, and saying to himself, as he passed every milestone, "So much nearer New York." About a mile out in the country he came to a large farmhouse, and he determined to enter and ask for a meal. He had hard work to muster up enough courage to go in and ask for anything, but finally he knocked timidly at the kitchen door, and was frightened by a large dog which came barking around the corner. It seemed to him that the animal would surely bite, but a large fat woman opened the door just in time to let him in. "Hurry in, boy," she said, "fer there's no tellin' what Tige might do ef he once gets a hold of ye." So Archie stepped into the large kitchen, with its rafters overhead, and its dining-table in the corner. "Sit down, boy," said the woman. "I reckon you's thet new lad thet's come ter work over at Mullins's, ain't ye?"

"No'm," said Archie, "I don't work anywhere. I'm on my way to New York, where I expect to find a position, and I thought perhaps you'd allow me to do a little work here this morning to earn my breakfast."

Good Mrs. Lane, for that was the woman's name, was horrified to think that any one was alive and without breakfast at eight o'clock in the morning. "Goodness me!" said she. "Why, you must be half-famished fer want of food, ain't ye?" And she bustled about the kitchen, putting the kettle on to boil, and stirring up the fire. "You'll have some nice ham and eggs, my boy, and then I have somethin' in mind fer you. I reckon yer ain't in no hurry ter get ter the city, be ye? Well, even if ye do be in a hurry, I reckon you'll be glad of the chance to earn four dollars. I ain't goin' to ask ye no questions about how ye come to be walkin' to New York, because I never wuz no hand ter meddle in other folkses affairs, but ye look to be a likely lad, and a strong un, and ez my sister's husband, what lives two miles down the pike, needs a boy to drive a plough fer a week, I b'lieve ye'll suit 'im first-rate. So ez soon ez ye have finished yer vittles, I'll walk down there with ye, and we'll see the old man."

Archie hardly knew whether to be delighted with the prospect or not. Of course four dollars would be nice to have, but he was anxious to get to the city as soon as possible, and every day counted. But perhaps it would be wrong, he thought, to throw away such a good chance to earn some money, and he had decided to accept any offer the farmer made him, long before he finished his breakfast. When he got up from the straight-backed chair, he felt that he had never eaten a better meal in his life, and when Mrs. Lane started off down the road, he gladly followed her. A week on such a farm as this would be no unpleasant experience. Such food was not to be had every day, he knew, and he of course would have precious little that was good to eat when he reached the city.

They soon covered the two miles, Mrs. Lane getting along very fast for such a large woman, and at last they stood before Hiram Tinch, who owned the farm. Archie was made to describe his intentions, and was thoroughly examined by Mr. Tinch. He told the farmer that he knew nothing about farm work, but Mr. Tinch said he would soon teach him, and it was settled that Archie was to remain on the farm a week. Mrs. Lane went inside the house to see her sister, who looked sick with too much work, and the farmer told Archie that he might as well start in, as there was no object in waiting. So the boy donned a pair of "blue jean" trousers, and was taken into a field, where a one-horse plough was standing. Archie knew how to hitch a horse, so he went to the stable and secured his steed, and then harnessed him to the plough. The farmer didn't see fit to give him any instructions about ploughing, and the poor boy hardly knew what to do, but rather than ask he started off, and tried to guide the animal in the right direction, as far as he knew it. Of course the horse went wrong, and the plough refused to stay in the earth, and altogether the attempt was a miserable failure. The farmer leaned against the fence, picking his teeth with a pin, but when he saw the horse going crooked, and the plough bounding along over the earth, his face grew livid with anger. For a minute he seemed unable to speak, but strode toward Archie with a fierce look in his eyes. Then he found his tongue, and opened such a tirade of vile words that the poor boy shrank from him in terror. He was in mortal fear lest the man should lay hands on him and commit some crime, so intense was his rage, but Hiram Tinch seemed to know how far to go, and after five minutes of cursing and swearing he took the plough in his own hands, and guided it through the earth. "Now take it," he growled at Archie, when he had gone a furrow's length, "and see ef ye can do better this time. Remember, not a bite of dinner do ye get until this field is ploughed."

Poor Archie was weak from fright, but there was nothing to do but to obey. He looked at the vast field before him, and made up his mind that he would get nothing to eat until night, anyhow, for it was already nearly noon. He felt very much like bursting into tears, but he was too proud to give way to his feelings. But he couldn't help wishing that he were at home, playing with the members of the Hut Club. "Those boys are much better off than I am," he said, over and over, "though they have made no effort to improve themselves." After a time, however, his ambition returned, and as he looked ahead into the future, and remembered the wonderful things he was going to accomplish, he felt more like working.

He finished the field at five o'clock in the afternoon, and was almost fainting from hunger and from the hard work. The ploughing was fairly well done, but Hiram Tinch could see no merit in the work. He swore at Archie again, and gave him a supper of mush and milk. Mrs. Tinch sat by, and Archie could see that she did not approve of his treatment. The poor woman seemed afraid to speak, almost, but it was plain that she had a good heart. So when Archie heard a noise in his garret room that night, he was not surprised to see Mrs. Tinch at the window, placing some doughnuts and sandwiches there for him to eat.

CHAPTER V.

THE NIGHT AMONG THE RUINS--THE CAMP-FIRE OF THE TRAMPS.

IT seemed to Archie that he had just fallen asleep when old Hiram Tinch was shaking him awake. "Git up out o' here now, ye lazy beggar, and git to the field and finish that there ploughin'," he growled, and the frightened lad awakened from a horrible nightmare, only to find a worse experience awaiting him in the light of day. He hastily drew on his trousers, and didn't wait to don either shoes or stockings, for if he was to spend the day ploughing in a field, he knew he would be more comfortable in his bare feet. When he reached the kitchen, he found that Farmer Tinch had already eaten his breakfast, though it was not daylight. Archie was glad that he was out of the way, and good Mrs. Tinch was glad of it, too, for she was able to give the boy a good breakfast, and some good advice with it. "Don't you pay no attention to what my man says, laddie. He's a powerful man to swear and carry on, but I don't think he'll have the meanness to strike you. Ef he does, ye must come to me, and I'll see thet he doesn't do it no more."

Archie was grateful for this spirit of friendliness, but in his heart he thought that cruel words were often more painful than lashes, and he heartily wished that his week was over.

All this day he spent on the farm, without once going into the road. Farmer Tinch had warned him that if he saw him making for the road at any time, he could go and never come back, and he would forfeit what money he had already earned. So Archie ploughed the field from daylight till dark, with a half hour at noon for a hurried dinner. He was glad when darkness came, and after another supper of mush and milk he was thankful to have a corn-husk bed to sleep on, and was soon in a stupor which was so sound as to be almost like death.

Again the next morning he was awakened at daylight, and he was made to work even harder than on the second day. He had by this time become somewhat used to the labour, however, and stood it better. He was more successful in his work, too, and Farmer Tinch had less opportunity for cursing him. But at night he seemed more tired, even, than before, and he longed for his home again. He thought of the cosy bed he would now be enjoying if he had only taken his mother's advice, and he felt almost like getting up in the night and stealing away on the road to the north. But, always a sensible lad, Archie realised that this discouragement could not last, and he lost himself in sleep, looking forward three days, when his week should be up, and he would be on his way to the city, with four dollars more to add to his slender store.

The three days passed slowly, but at length the Saturday night came, and he prepared to be off. But good Mrs. Tinch entreated him to remain with them over Sunday, and, as Archie wasn't sure that it would be quite right for him to travel on Sunday, he decided to do so. So the next day he brushed his only suit of clothes, and drove with his late employer to church, where Farmer Tinch sat in a front seat and passed the bread and wine at communion. Archie's heart rose to his throat as he saw this paragon so devout in church. He felt like rising in his seat and denouncing him before all the people as a tyrant and a hard-hearted wretch. But he kept quiet, though he found it impossible to partake of the communion under such circumstances.

The Tinches had brought their dinner with them, and at noon they all sat on one of the grassy mounds in the churchyard, to take some refreshment before the afternoon service began. When they had finished, Archie wandered off, and came to a crowd of boys who were romping behind the church. When they saw him approach, they all stopped their noise, and looked at him wonderingly. Evidently they were not used to seeing strange boys. The silence was soon broken, however, by one of the boys calling out, "Why, fellers, thet's the chap what's been workin' fer Hiram Tinch." This announcement was enough to make Archie an even greater object of interest than before, for the boys seemed to think that any person who could work for Farmer Tinch, and come out of the ordeal none the worse for wear, must be something wonderful. Archie was soon on good terms with them all, however, and told them of his plan of going to New York. The boys were all attention, and soon he was the hero of the occasion. When the bell rung for the afternoon service he was still telling them of the things he was going to do, and none of them wanted to go into the church. Archie persuaded them to enter, however, but he was not surprised to meet them all along the road when he left Tinch's early Monday morning.

It was almost time to go to bed when they reached the farmhouse that night, so Archie went at once to his attic, being anxious to start fresh on his journey the next day. He was now determined to push on as rapidly as possible, hoping to reach the city within three or four days. He was somewhat afraid that he wouldn't be able to do this, but he was going to try, anyhow.

At daylight Monday morning he was on the way, and when the various boys he met the day before said good-bye to him and wished him good luck, he felt that his stay at Tinch's had not been without benefits of some sort. He had made some boy friends, and he was four dollars richer, Archie was sensible enough, too, to realise that his experience would be a valuable one to him in the future. He knew now what hard work was, at any rate.

The morning walk was delightful. The September weather was perfect, and all along the road were fruit-trees laden with every sort of good thing to eat a boy could wish for. And as the trees were on the public thoroughfare, Archie did net hesitate to help himself freely as he went along, so that he didn't require any meal at noon.

As night drew near, however, he began to wonder what he would do for a bed, and the question became more important with every hour. He had come to no towns since morning, and knew that he couldn't expect to reach one of any size until the next day, anyhow. There were farmhouses, of course, but after his experience of the past week the lad felt that he would rather remain outdoors all night than risk being thrown in with another Hiram Tinch. He didn't know enough of farmers to know that few of them resemble Mr. Tinch in nature, and he did what he thought was best in keeping away from farmhouses after this.

It was five o'clock in the evening, and Archie was beginning to feel very tired and hungry, when he came to the ruins of an old colonial mansion, which lay far back from the road, surrounded by trees, and almost hid with shrubbery. "How interesting," he thought to himself. "It looks just like the pictures of old ruins we see in geographies. I think I must go up and see what they look like at close range." And, fired with a spirit of adventure, and making believe that he was an explorer in an ancient country, the boy made his way through the trees and shrubbery. The ruins looked more and more interesting as he advanced. This had evidently been a magnificent estate at one time. There were massive pillars which had once supported a stately portico at the front of the house, and above all there rose a massive chimney, which seemed to be exceedingly well preserved. As Archie came nearer, he was surprised to notice a thin column of smoke rising from the top of the chimney, and for a moment he stood still with fright. What could this mean? Who could be building a fire in the midst of these ruins. It was almost like what one reads about in books, he thought.

For some time he could not decide what to do, whether he had better keep on, or whether the wisest policy would be to get back to the road as quickly as possible. Finally, his curiosity and thirst for adventure persuaded him to go on, and he continued to push his way through the shrubbery until he stood before the ruins. He then climbed a flight of steps, and stood in what had once been the main entrance to this massive palace. Before him he saw a scene which was almost weird in its unusualness. A fire of pine-knots was blazing in the ruins of the great fireplace, and seated in a semicircle around the fire were several men of picturesque appearance, whose faces looked up angrily when they were disturbed.

CHAPTER VI.

STEALING A RIDE--KICKED OUT BY THE BRAKEMAN.

ARCHIE was dumbfounded. Never before had he been among such a motley crowd, and his first impulse was to turn and run. But on second thought he decided that it would be best to put on a bold face and walk up to the men. This he did, and when he reached the fire the men jumped up and asked him who he was. In a few words he told them his simple story, and they all laughed and sat down again about the fire, making a place for him. "You're one of us, then, laddie," said the leader of the gang. "We're all soldiers of fortune, all dependent upon the generous public for our livelihood. But we're not goin' to the city. There's nothin' there for us, and our advice to you is for you to steer clear of the place, too. Them police takes ye and throws ye into jail as quick as a wink, and there's no chance of gettin' anythink to eat at basement doors, neither. They're all on to us, there, laddie, and ye'd better stick to the country."

This bit of advice was endorsed by the entire company, and it was in vain that Archie tried to make them understand that he was no ordinary tramp, walking about the country in search of an easy time. He tried to tell them that he was going to the city to work, not to beg; but the leader, a big, dirty fellow, weighing two hundred pounds or over, said, "Never mind, laddie, we knows you've run away from home to get away from the folks, and we appreciates yer position. If yer a mind to stand by us, we'll stand by you, and see thet ye comes to no harm."

On thinking things over, Archie decided that it was perhaps the wisest thing for him to appear to sympathise with the tramps, and make himself agreeable while with them. He had undoubtedly run into a gang of the worst sort of vagabonds, and there was no way of getting away from there without arousing their suspicions. So he partook of their slender meal, and joined in the general laughter when the leader, "Fattie Foy," made some crude attempt at punning. The meal was one to be remembered. The coffee had been heated in an empty tomato can over the fire, and from its taste was evidently a combination of various collections made from the farmhouses round about. Besides the coffee there was a various collection of sandwiches and bread and butter, and two pieces of cake. One man had succeeded in striking a good house, and came back laden with pickles and crackers and cheese, which were probably the remains of some picnic basket. Another fellow had brought some pieces of cold bacon, and these were warmed on sticks over the fire until they looked really appetising. From some barn had come a half-dozen fresh eggs, and these were quickly boiled in a can of hot water, and made a very fair showing on the slab of granite which served as a table.

When everything was ready the provisions were equally divided among the crowd, and every one shared alike. It made no difference how much more one man collected than another, it was always shared with the entire crowd. Poor Archie found it almost impossible to eat, but the men insisted that he take something, so he did manage to swallow a few sips of coffee and eat a slice of bread and butter. But as he looked about him at the dirty hands and faces, and the filthy garments of the tramps, he determined not to eat again while with them.

When the meal was over the two tin cans were washed at a spring of water, and as it was now quite dark, they all sat close to the fire, in order to see. Some one produced a pack of dirty cards, and they began a game of some kind. Archie was asked to join, but he told them he didn't know anything about card-playing. The poor lad was beginning to wish he had never left home, and felt more miserable than at any other period of the journey. He walked over to a corner of the ruins where the light from the fire did not penetrate, and, once there, he sat down and sobbed bitterly for a time. When he had finished crying it seemed impossible for him to sleep. The scene about the fire fascinated him. The men were seated in every sort of picturesque attitude, and as the flickering light fell upon their dark faces it wasn't hard for the poor lad to imagine that he had fallen among a crowd of brigands. He watched them as they played until he could see no longer, and then he fell into a sound sleep.

When Archie woke it was still dark, but the moon was shining brightly overhead, making everything as light as day. He rubbed his eyes and sat up, and it was some time before he could realise where he was. Then, as he saw the tramps lying about the ground, he remembered his adventures of the night before, and, horrified that he had allowed himself to sleep, he hastily jumped up, and determined to get away from the ruins as quickly as possible. The tramps were all sleeping soundly, and the only noises to be heard were the sound of their breathing and the blood-curdling hoot of some owl perched on the pillars of the old portico. The boy picked his way carefully between the bodies of the sleeping men, and in a minute stood once more on the grand flight of steps outside. He was trembling for fear some tramp would awake and prevent his going, and when a bat brushed him in its flight he almost screamed with terror. Far out beyond the trees and the shrubby he could see the road glistening in the moonlight, and he made his way as rapidly as possible out of the grounds, and was once more on his way to the city.

It was lonesome work, walking along a country road at night, and Archie remembered with longing his cosy bed at home. The feeling of homesickness kept growing within him, despite his efforts to down it, and when at last the glorious autumn sun rose over the eastern horizon he was miserable with longing for mother and for home. But he was too proud to even think of turning back. He must reach the city at all hazards, homesick or not.

Archie did not think of breakfast this morning. His experience of the night before seemed to have taken away his appetite entirely, and his only thought was to walk as fast as possible, so that he could reach the city soon. About nine o'clock he entered the outskirts of a busy town, and while there he observed that the railroad going to the city passed through the place. All at once a new idea occurred to him. He had so often heard men and boys tell of how they had stolen a ride from one town to another. Why shouldn't he be able to get a ride on a freight train to the city. Would it be wrong? Archie thought not, since so many men did it. And anyhow it didn't seem a wicked thing to cheat the railroad. He had heard people say that the company ought to be cheated whenever possible, since it cheated so many others. So, from being so tired and so anxious to reach New York, Archie decided to try and steal a ride. He entered the yards, where a train was being made up for the south, and there he saw a cattle-car with an open door. He immediately jumped inside and shut the door, squeezing himself into the farthest corner, hoping that he wouldn't be discovered. He soon found that he wasn't alone, for a couple of tramps were in the opposite corner, and they whispered to him not to make any noise. "The brakie," they said, "will soon be 'round, and if he finds ye he'll put us all in jail."

Poor Archie grew pale at the thought of being put in jail, and huddled himself closer in the corner. After a time the train started, and the tramps, he noticed, climbed up into some sort of compartment under the roof of the car, where they wouldn't be observed, leaving Archie alone down-stairs. Things went smoothly for a time. The train went flying along, and Archie counted every mile which brought him nearer to the city. Finally the train pulled up at a crossing, and a brakeman came along and threw open the door of the car. He was not long in discovering the cowering figure in the corner, and his wrath was dreadful to look upon. "So, ye cussed vagabond," he growled, "ye thought ye'd steal a ride, did ye? Get out o' this now. Quick, out with ye." Archie could have fainted, and, as it was, he almost fell out of the car, propelled by the brakeman's boot. For awhile he stood dazed beside the track, and finally moved on. "I'll keep a 'stiff upper lip,'" he said, "whatever happens." But this was by far the most discouraging adventure yet.

CHAPTER VII.

ARRIVAL IN NEW YORK--A NIGHT IN A LODGING-HOUSE.

ON and on for the rest of the day walked Archie. His feet were sore, he was weak from hunger, and he was made miserable with being home-sick. People who met him on the road turned around to look at the slender lad with the pale face and the weary step, but he kept walking on, stopping for nothing, and noticing no one. At noon he picked some apples in an orchard, and these appeased his hunger. When evening drew near, however, he felt that he could go without food no longer, so he didn't hesitate to stop at a house and ask for food. "I know mother would give a boy food if one should come to our door," he said to himself, "so I do not think it wrong for me to ask for food here." He was fortunate enough to strike a pleasant housewife, who took him in and made him sit down at the kitchen table, which she covered with good things to eat. There was cold roast beef, some fried potatoes and a glass of good fresh milk. And then she gave him some apple pie, so that when he had finished Archie felt better than for many a day. While he ate he told the good woman why he was going to New York, and her sympathy was enlisted at once. "Why, you poor lad," she exclaimed, "just to think of your being in the city all alone. And what will your mother think?"

Archie couldn't imagine what his mother did think. He had remembered her every minute during the last few days, and was anxious to write her, so he decided to ask the woman for some paper and a pencil. These were gladly given him, and he sat down and told his mother that he was almost to New York and that he had been having a splendid time. He was careful not to say anything about his experience with Farmer Tinch, or the night he spent with the tramps. He knew these things would only make her unhappy, and it was just as well that she should think everything was smooth sailing for him. His letter was filled with his enthusiasm and his hope for the morrow, so that when good Mrs. Dunn received it she was overjoyed, and hurried over to show it to the Widow Sullivan, who enjoyed it thoroughly and said "I told you so." Poor Mrs. Dunn had been having a very miserable time of it. She was hardly surprised that morning when she awoke and found Archie gone, but she was naturally much worried for fear some accident would happen to him before he reached New York. Once there, she felt that she needn't worry much about him, for, strange to say, Mrs. Dunn had a firm belief in the ability of city policemen to take care of every one, and she knew that Archie would not be allowed to suffer for want of food and a place to sleep. And when she received this letter, saying that Archie was nearly to New York, and had even been so successful as to earn some money, she felt more comfortable than for some time, Of course she supposed that he would be home before long. She was positive that he wouldn't be able to get any work in the city, and knew that as soon as his money gave out he would return. "It's all for the best," she said to Mrs. Sullivan. "The habit of running away from home was born in the boy. His father left home when he was no older than Archie, and no harm ever came to him. So I'm not going to worry, Mrs. Sullivan." And then Mrs. Dunn would go back to her home, and at sight of Archie's old hat or some of his football paraphernalia, would burst into tears.

The good woman who gave Archie his supper refused to let him start out again on the road that night. She told him that he must remain with them, for they had an extra bed up over the kitchen which was never needed, and that he might just as well sleep there as not. So for the first time in nearly a week Archie slept comfortably, and, as he heard the familiar sounds in the kitchen below him in the morning, it was hard for him to make up his mind that he was not at home, and that it was not his mother who was grinding the coffee in the kitchen below. He heard the ham frying in the skillet, and the rattle of the dishes as his hostess set the table, and then he dressed himself and hastened downstairs, feeling ready for a good day's walking.

When he had eaten his breakfast he started out again. The woman told him that it was only about fifteen miles to New York, and that after he had walked about six of them he could take a trolley-car and ride the remainder of the distance for five cents. So he thanked her for her kindness, and promised to let her know how he succeeded in the city, for the woman was much interested in his future. He felt almost sorry to leave the home-like place, but the prospect of reaching the city this very day was enough to make him anxious to be off. He covered the six miles to the trolley-car before eleven o'clock in the morning, and then in an hour and a quarter more the trolley landed him in lower New York.

His sensations as he was whirled along the smooth pavements, past beautiful buildings and handsome residences, may be better imagined than described. After looking forward to this day for so long, he was almost overcome at the realisation of his hopes, and took the utmost delight in everything about him. When the car stopped at the terminus of the line, he got out and walked up the busiest street in the neighbourhood. He hardly knew what to do first, but continued walking until he came to the New York end of the great Brooklyn Bridge. Then he couldn't resist the desire to walk across the bridge, and he started out upon the journey. Up the steps he walked, and soon he had climbed as far as the middle of the magnificent structure. There he stood for some time, looking out over Governor's Island, nestled like a green egg in a nest of red buildings, and past Staten Island to the open sea beyond It was all grander, more beautiful than anything he had ever seen before, and he felt glad that he had come. Then in another direction he saw the never-ending succession of buildings, some tall, some low ones, but all inhabited with swarms of people. "There are three million people in this great city," he said to himself, "and over them in New Jersey, in those cities I see, there are a million more, and I am one of four million." The thought was too much for the boy, and he continued his walk across the bridge. Once across, he came back again, for Brooklyn was a strange place to him. In New York City he felt more at home, for he had at least spent two days within its limits.

Once back in the busy streets, he decided to look about for a cheap place to stay for the night. It was the middle of the afternoon now, and he felt that he ought to make some preparation. He knew better than to apply at the police station for lodging, for he knew they would probably turn him over to the famous Gerry Society, which would send him back home before a day had passed, and then where would his ambitions be?

He remembered the place where he had stayed with Uncle Henry, but he knew that this would be too high-priced for his pocketbook, so he started up the Bowery, where he expected to find some very cheap places. He didn't like the looks of the people he met in the street, but his experiences on the way to New York had taught him not to be too particular about a little dirt. So when he came to a rickety building with a sign up, "Beds, ten and fifteen cents," he immediately went up the dark, filthy stairway, and found himself in a large room at the top which served as the "hotel" office. There were rows of chairs in front of the windows and along the walls, and in the chairs were the queerest-looking lot of men he had ever seen. He didn't pay any attention to them, though, but went up to the seedy individual behind the desk, and asked him if he could get a bed for the night. "Sure, Mike," the man replied, and Archie signed his name in a dirty book with torn pages. He paid the man ten cents, and asked if he could leave his bundle while he went outside. "Sure, Mike," was again his answer, and the man took his little bundle of necessities and threw them on the floor behind the counter. When Archie had gone out, a fat man with a baby face came up and whispered to the clerk. "Anything in the bloke?" he inquired. "Nit," said the clerk, "don't yer see his baggage? Does it look like there's anything in it?" And the mysterious conversation closed, to be continued later in the evening.

CHAPTER VIII.

LOOKING FOR WORK--WASHING DISHES IN A BOWERY
RESTAURANT.

FTER a couple of hours spent in going about the streets, Archie went
into a place where he bought some coffee and rolls for his supper. He
paid only five cents for three sweet rolls and a large cup of coffee which
was not at all bad to taste, and he returned to the lodging-house on the
Bowery feeling better than he had expected to feel when he started out from the
homestead where he spent the previous night, If he could get a good meal for five
or ten cents, and could sleep for ten cents more, he would have enough to keep him
going for some time.

The Bowery at night presented a wonderful appearance to Archie's mind. The
brilliantly lighted shops, the cheap theatres with their bands of musicians on the
sidewalk in front of the entrance, were all attractive to his boyish eyes, but he was
wise enough to pass them all by, and to make his way as quickly as possible to the
cheap lodging-house. The street was jammed with persons of every description.
He was surprised particularly at the number of Chinamen he met, for he didn't
know that a block or two away was the centre of the Chinese population of New
York, where the Celestials have their theatre, their hotels, their great stores, and
their joss-house. There were many Italians in the street, too, and Polish Jews, to say
nothing of Frenchmen and Germans. Then there was the typical Bowery "tough,"
who swaggered up and down, looking for trouble, which he usually finds before an
evening passes. Archie was not afraid in this cosmopolitan crowd. No one seemed
to notice him, and, anyhow, there were a great many policemen about, who seemed
to keep a sharp lookout all the time. And as Archie shared his mother's faith in the

city policeman, he felt no fear.

In the lodging-house everything looked very much as before. The chairs were still occupied with filthy-looking men, who smoked and spat and talked in under-tones among themselves. The boy paid no attention to any of them, but, walking up to the seedy individual behind the counter, asked him if he could go to bed now. The man answered, "Certainly," and sent a fellow with Archie to show him his bed. It was in a long, narrow room, which was poorly lighted with a few gas-jets here and there, and which was filled with about thirty beds, all narrow, and all dirty. One of these was pointed out to Archie, and then the man left him. The poor lad felt more homesick than ever, and had it not been that he had a glorious to-morrow to look forward to, he would have been very miserable indeed. As it was, he undressed and got between the chilly sheets, when he remembered that he hadn't looked after his little roll of bills for a long time, and that some of them might be missing. He crawled out of bed again, and felt inside the lining of his coat for the purse. He had sewed it there for safe-keeping until he reached the city, for he had some little change in his pocket, which he knew would last him for several days.

The poor boy's hand felt nothing but a cut in the lining, where the roll of bills had been, and all at once he realised that the money must have been stolen from him. And he at once thought of the night in the ruins, when he fell asleep among the tramps, and there was no doubt in his mind but that they had taken his money from him. This was a terrible blow. Here he was, with just a few cents in his pocket, and no one to whom he could appeal for aid. It was the worst predicament Archie had ever been in, and he hardly knew what to do. He sat on the side of his dirty little bed for awhile, and then he snuggled under the covers and was soon asleep again. For a boy who has been walking all day seldom stays awake from worry.

But when he awoke in the morning, it was to realise the fact that he must get some money this very day or go to the police station. The few cents he had remain-ing were only enough to buy some coffee and bread for breakfast, and the poor lad didn't know where his next meal would come from. As he went out, the clerk in the filthy office of the lodging-house told him that he needn't come back any more.

"Why did you tell him that?" asked the fat man with a sly face.

"Because I went through his clothes last night when he was asleep, and he had only six cents in his pocket. We don't want no starvin' brats around here, to bring the Gerry Society down upon us."

It was well that Archie didn't know his pockets had been searched while he was asleep, or his faith in human nature would have been more shaken than ever before. He had not suspected that the men in this lodging-house might be dishonest.

"They are poor," he said to himself when he saw them first, "but they may be good men for all that."

After a slender meal, Archie found a library where he looked over the advertising columns of the morning papers, trying to find some position open which he thought he might fill. There were several advertisements calling for office boys, and all these he made note of, and then as he looked down the page he noticed that a boy was wanted in a restaurant to wash dishes. He decided that if he didn't succeed in getting a place as office boy, he might get the restaurant place. He knew that in a restaurant he would be likely at least to get enough to eat.

For two hours he called at addresses of men who wanted office boys, but at every place he was turned away. "We have already hired one," some of them said, and others told him that they never took any boys in the office who were living away from home. Some asked him for recommendations, and when he had none, they looked at him and told him "good morning." It was all terribly discouraging, and with every minute Archie was wishing more and more that he were back home again. Somehow the city seemed different now from what it had been when Uncle Henry was with him. Everything was less bright, and the things he had been delighted with before were less interesting now.

Finally, he entered a large, handsome suite of rooms, in one of the great skyscrapers, and was shown into a very elegant private office. There he found an old gentleman seated in a great easy chair, looking over papers, and keeping one eye upon a buzzing instrument at his side which seemed to be spitting out long strips of paper, like a magician in a side-show. The man looked up as he entered, and cleared his throat. "Ahem," he said, "you look as if you were from the country. I wonder, now, if you have came to the city to seek your fortune."

Archie was embarrassed. "Yes, sir, I suppose you might put it that way," he replied.

"Well," continued the old gentleman, "my advice to you is to go back where you came from as quickly as you can. Not one boy in a thousand will gain either fame or fortune in New York, and you stand a wonderful chance of sinking lower every year. And even if you do succeed, you will miss many beautiful things in your life which may come to you in the country. You can have a pleasant home there, and live an easy, natural life, while here it will be years before you can expect to accomplish much, and you will spend your life in a nervous strain. Think well, young man, before choosing the great city as your sphere of usefulness."

"I've made up my mind, sir," said Archie. "I have quite decided to remain in the city."

"Very well," said the old gentleman, "I hope you may never regret it. But we have already hired an office boy. Good morning."

Archie walked out, more discouraged than ever. Perhaps, after all, a country life was not to be so much despised. This man ought to know what he was talking about. But once outside, in the Broadway crowd, Archie forgot everything about the country, and was lost in the delight of being one of four million.

He now decided to accept the place in the restaurant, if it were not taken, and, fortunately for him, it was not. So he rolled up his sleeves, and began to wash dishes as if he had done nothing else in all his life before.

CHAPTER IX.

IN THE STREET AGAIN--THE POLICE STATION--VISITS THE
NEWSPAPER OFFICE, AND IS KINDLY RECEIVED BY THE EDITOR.

ALL day long Archie washed dishes, and before night came he decided that he had never before had such discouraging work. The restaurant was a popular one, and there were very many dishes to be washed, to say nothing of the pots and pans which were always dirty. Archie no sooner finished one sink full of dishes than another large pile was waiting to be put through the same operation, and there was no time at all for looking about him. There was hardly time for eating, even, and at noon he was only able to snatch a few mouthfuls. The work was not interesting, and it was a new sort of labour to Archie, so that altogether he did not get on as well as he might have wished. The cook was constantly nagging him, and telling him to hurry up, and the poor lad tried his best to please him. But somehow everything went wrong, and he was hardly surprised when the proprietor came in at six o'clock with a new man for the place. "Come around in the morning," he said to Archie, "and I'll pay your day's wages."

So the boy was in the street once more, with no money, and no place to sleep. He wasn't hungry, that was one thing, for he had been allowed to eat a good meal before leaving the restaurant. But where was he to sleep, and what was he to do on the morrow, when he would surely be hungry? His experience at looking for work had not been encouraging, and he began to have serious doubts as to whether he would ever get a place. Certainly he would starve if he waited around New York long without anything to do.

It was quite dark at seven o'clock, and Archie walked over to the brilliantly lighted street which ran north and south through the city. He had never failed to find something interesting to look at there, and he felt now that he would like to see the bright side of city life, even if he couldn't enjoy it himself. So all the evening he walked up and down the street, watching the well-dressed crowds hurrying into the theatres and the other almost innumerable places of amusement. He stared in open-mouthed amazement at some of the costumes of the women he saw alighting from carriages. Never before had he seen anything half so beautiful, and if any one had told him that there were such dresses he would have told them he didn't believe it. Some of them, he thought, must cost hundreds of dollars, and the jewels worn with them many hundreds more. How interesting, how new, it all was to him! Once he thought of the little home in the village, and at first wished that his mother might be there to enjoy the sights with him. "But I wouldn't want her to see me," he thought, "not while I am so miserable, and feeling so discouraged." For Archie was beginning to wonder if he hadn't made a mistake in leaving home, whether he had not been overconfident and hot-headed. But he decided to try it a few days more, that is, if he could manage to live for that length of time in the city.

At twelve o'clock he was walking up and down the street, which was still bright with millions of lights, though the crowds had gone home from the theatres, and the restaurants were beginning to be less popular. He was still wondering how he was going to find a place to sleep, when he was accosted by a policeman, and taken into a doorway. "I've been watching you," said the officer, "and I want to know why you are walking up and down the street at this time of night."

Archie could have cried from fright, but he remembered that he was under suspicion, so decided to tell the policeman his whole story, and perhaps he could help him out in some way. So he described his experiences during the day, and was surprised at the interest shown by the officer in the recital. When he had finished he was told that he would be taken to the police station. "You needn't be afraid, my lad," said the policeman. "I'll see that the Gerry Society doesn't get you and send you home, that is, if you think you want to try it here a few days longer. You can sleep at the station to-night, and the next morning you can try it again." So to the station they went, and Archie was, naturally, a little frightened when he saw, for the first time, the cells, and the terribly severe appearance of all his surroundings. But he was given a good bed in which to sleep, and he passed a delightful night, dreaming of the wonderful adventures which befell him in the city.

He was not awakened until eight o'clock, and then he found the good policeman waiting to take him out to breakfast, He expressed surprise that he should be so kind to him.

"I always thought that officers were cross and unpleasant," he said, "but you're not that kind, anyhow."

"Well," laughed the officer, "we have to be cross very often, though we're sometimes sorry to be so. But I've taken a fancy to you, my lad. I like to see a boy who does things. When a boy of seventeen is willing to come to New York alone, and make his own way, without friends or influence of any kind, it shows a proper spirit, and he ought to succeed. I know you'll get along if you only persevere. I'd advise you to keep on trying."

"Oh, I'm going to, now," said Archie. "I was very homesick and discouraged last night, but since I've met you I seem to have received a new impetus, and I'm ready to make a new beginning."

So Archie and the policeman parted friends.

"Come around to the station to-night if you want a bed, and you shall be cared for," said the officer, as he turned around the corner into the busy street, where he was lost in the crowd.

Archie walked down the street, hardly knowing what to do first. He didn't feel like answering any more advertisements in the newspapers, and he decided to go into a few stores and ask for work. He was about to do this when he saw before him the magnificent building of the New York Enterprise. It was a truly beautiful structure, rising fifteen stories above the ground, and surmounted with an artistic tower, which could be seen from almost any part of the city. The home of the city's greatest daily, it looked as if it were always welcoming strangers to the metropolis, and Archie felt an irresistible impulse to enter. Everything connected with a newspaper had for him the greatest fascination, and he knew he would enjoy seeing through this wonderful building, which was almost wholly occupied by the departments of the Enterprise. So he entered the door, and passed from one floor to another, finally arriving at the highest floor of all, where were located the editorial rooms of the Evening Enterprise. All at once a new plan entered Archie's fertile brain. Why shouldn't he be able to get something to do on a newspaper? It had always been his greatest ambition to become a reporter, and here, although he didn't think the editor would take him in that capacity, he thought he might get some sort of work in which he could work himself up.

There upon the door were the magic words: "Editor of the Evening enterprise. No Admittance." Archie opened the door and entered. He knew it would be useless to send in his name. It was best to see the editor at once, and without ceremony. He was seated before a large desk, which was littered with papers of every description, and he was a very pleasant person in appearance. Archie stood hesitating near the door, and remained there a minute or two before the editor looked up.

"Well, my boy, what is it?"

Archie took courage.

"I--I want to be a reporter, sir, and I thought it would do no harm to ask you for such a position, anyhow."

The distinguished journalist wheeled about in his chair.

"What!" he exclaimed, "you want to be a reporter. Why, my dear boy, how old are you?"

"I'll be eighteen my next birthday," said Archie, "and, sir, I've had some experiences in the last two weeks, which make me feel as if I were about five years older than I really am. I've been through some very trying experiences, sir."

The editor was interested at once. "Tell me what your experiences have been," he said, and Archie began, and told him his whole story; how he had left home to win fame and fortune, and how he had worked on the farm for a week with Farmer Tinch; how he had been robbed the night he stayed with the tramps in the ancient ruins, and how he had finally reached the city. Then he told him of the night in the lodging-house, of his dish-washing experience in the restaurant, and how he had been taken from the street by a policeman the night before, and allowed to sleep in the station-house. When he had finished the editor had a broad grin upon his face.

"By Jove!" he exclaimed, "this is certainly rich stuff. There's a good story in it, I'll be bound."

Then, speaking to Archie, he said:

"Just wait here a minute, my boy, and I'll see if we can't put some money in your way."

He pressed a button at the side of his desk, and when a boy appeared, he told him to bring "Mr. Jones, please, or one of the other reporters. And tell Jones to bring an artist with him."

The reporter and the artist soon stood before the editor, who told them, with great glee, that he had a leading feature for the next evening edition of the Enterprise. "Just talk to this boy, Jones, and see if you can't make two good columns on the front page and two for the inside from his story. I think it's great, myself. And you Cash," he said, turning to the artist, "you make a good sketch of the boy."

Archie could hardly believe his eyes and ears. Just to think that he was being interviewed, and that his picture was to be in the paper. It seemed almost too good to be true.

When the reporter had finished with him, he was taken down-stairs to the cashier's office and given thirty dollars in bills. "This will pay you for the interview," said the editor, "and give you enough to fix up with. Now, to-morrow, you come in again, and I think I can give you steady employment."

Oh, how happy Archie was! He went out into the street, and seemed to fairly walk on air. Then he heard the newsboys crying, "Extra paper, read about the Enterprise's Boy Reporter." And when Archie saw the paper, there on the front page was his picture, together with the story of his "startling adventures."

CHAPTER X.

LIVING IN COMFORT AGAIN--FEATURED AS "THE BOY RE-PORTER."

ARCHIE often speaks of the day when he visited the newspaper office for the first time as the happiest day in all his life. The change from despair and homesickness to the joy of being appreciated by some one was so rapid that it made his head fairly swim with the exhilaration of success. With thirty dollars in his pocket, and the knowledge that he would have steady employment of the kind he desired on the morrow, he walked up the Bowery feeling like a prince. He entered the lodging-house where he had left his bundle of clothing, and so surprised the clerk by his new appearance that he was invited to remain there for another night. The shrewd man guessed that some good fortune must have befallen Archie, or he wouldn't be so happy. But the one night of misery which he had spent in the squalid hotel was enough for Archie, and he walked hastily uptown with his bundle, keeping a sharp lookout for a pleasant place where he might get a room. In his previous wanderings he had seen several nice houses with rooms to rent, but now that he wanted a room he found it difficult to find any of these neighbourhoods. He was anxious to get settled as quickly as possible, for he wanted to get everything done to-day, so that to-morrow he could have time to do anything required of him by the editor of the Enterprise. He must get a new suit of clothes, he must get his hair cut, and last, but not least, he must write home to mother and tell her of his great good fortune.

Finally, in his wanderings, Archie came to a beautiful square which was surrounded on every side by business houses and tenements. But the square itself and the houses on it were very quaint and very handsome, so that it seemed to be a very oasis in the desert. The green trees, just a little tinged with the brown and gold of autumn, reminded Archie of the front yard at home, and he decided to get a room in one of the houses here if he could possibly do so.

It so happened that there was a hall bedroom empty in one of the best-looking places, and Archie at once engaged it. The price was more reasonable than he had hoped for, even, and this made him happy, for as yet he had no idea how much his earnings would be, and he was anxious to be able to save something to send home, if he possibly could. The room was nicely furnished, and looked out upon the fountain, with the green trees, so that it was highly satisfactory in every respect. It didn't take Archie long to undo his bundle, and it was a pitiful display that greeted him when it was opened. The little comb and brush, a piece of soap, a Testament given him last Christmas by the teacher at Sunday school, a suit of underwear, and a couple of handkerchiefs. The whole lot of things hardly filled a corner in one of the bureau drawers, and Archie realised that he must buy a great many things within a week or two.

But before going out to do any shopping, he sat down and wrote a long letter home, describing his success of the morning, and telling his mother of the editor's promise to give him regular employment. He enclosed a copy of the paper with his picture and the story of his adventures, and it made him very happy to think of his mother's feelings when she read it all. Then, when he had finished, he went out to a post-office, and bought a money-order for ten dollars, which he also enclosed. "I know I can spare it," he said to himself, "and it will gratify her so much." Then, when the letter with its contents was safely mailed, he bought himself a new suit of clothing, and renovated himself in many ways, so that when he returned to his room in the square it was nearly dark, and he looked a different boy entirely.

Before going to bed, he determined to see his policeman friend, and tell him of his good fortune. "He is probably expecting me to sleep in the station," Archie thought, "and it will be a great surprise to him." But when he met the good man, he found that he had already heard of his success.

"I bought the Enterprise, and could hardly believe my eyes," said he, "but I always thought you would find some one to appreciate your pluck. I'm mighty glad for you, my lad, and you must always let me know how you are getting along." This Archie promised to do, and returned to his lodging to sleep.

The next morning he was on hand at the Enterprise office before the editor himself was down. The place was quite as fascinating as it had been on the preceding day, and he found something new to look at every minute. The reporters at their desks, several of whom introduced themselves and congratulated Archie on his perseverance, were a source of great interest to him, and the copy-boys, running here and there with special copy for the first edition, gave an air of hustling activity to the place that was very attractive to this new reporter.

When the editor came he had already thought of something for Archie to do. "Now you've been introduced to the public," he said, "and we want to feature you for a few days. Every one will be interested in knowing what you are doing, and what is going to become of you. You must write us an article for the paper to-day, telling about your experiences since yesterday, about getting a new suit, and about hunting for a room. And you can tell about your policeman friend, too."

This was surprising. Archie couldn't imagine why any one should be interested in knowing about his daily life, but he sat down and succeeded in writing a very interesting two columns about it. He was much surprised that he should be able to write so easily and so well. Of course he knew that composition and rhetoric had been his two strongest studies at school, but he had never realised before that he had any great talent for writing. When he had finished this article, the editor looked it over, and said, "That's great. You're all right, my boy. We'll make a great journalist of you yet," and of course this made Archie very happy. "Wait until this story is set up," said Mr. Jennings, the editor, "and I'll see what you can do in the way of correcting proofs."

When the proofs came, in a very short time, he hardly knew what to do with them. But in reading them he discovered several mistakes, which he lost no time in correcting, and Mr. Jennings said that he had done very well indeed. "Now you can spend the day in doing what you please. I would suggest that you go about New York and have as many strange experiences as possible, so that to-morrow you can write them up for us. And it will pay you, by the way, to go out to Coney Island, which is a different place from any you have seen before. You are sure to see some unusual things, and in the morning you can bring me in two columns about it."

Before leaving, Archie was asked if he needed any money. "You mustn't hesitate to ask for it, because you can have it as well to-day as on Saturday." But as he had left several dollars of the thirty he had received the day before, Archie didn't draw any more, and he thought it most remarkable that the editor should have so much money to pay out.

He had no difficulty in getting a trolley-car to Coney Island, and, after an hour's riding through Brooklyn streets, he found himself in the most unique and most delightful place imaginable, It was a queer-looking town, with great wheels in the air, high towers, with elevators and innumerable merry-go-rounds, and other sources of amusement. The noise was something terrific. Hand-organs, street-pianos, and German bands were all playing at the same time, while people hurried about from one place to another, enjoying the hundreds of games and riding the various scenic railways and carrousels. Archie stood mute with delight at it all, but before five minutes had passed he had shot the chutes, and had ridden over a steeplechase which took him through dark caverns, where dragons glared at him and where electrical sparks were constantly flying through the air. It was all so new, so different from anything he had seen before, that he was simply lost in admiration. He was standing near a theatre, when a short, dark man touched him on the arm, and said, "Come this way, young man, and I'll teach you the best game of all."

CHAPTER XI.

A DAY AND A NIGHT IN CONEY ISLAND--RAIDING A GAM-
BLING DEN.

ARCHIE was at first too much surprised to answer the man at all, but in a few moments he remembered that he was now a reporter, and that it was his duty to see all that he could, and have all the new experiences possible. So he decided to follow the man, and find out what "the best thing of all" in Coney Island was like. He was taken through several narrow alleyways, and finally he found himself in front of a tumble-down structure, built out directly over the water. It was very modest in appearance, and everything seemed quiet about the place. The shades were carefully drawn, and the dark man had to knock three times before the door was opened and they were permitted to enter. Inside, Archie found himself in a handsomely furnished apartment which differed greatly in appearance from the exterior of the building. There was a rich velvet carpet, mahogany furniture, and a great many small tables standing about the room. The place was filled with men, mostly well-dressed, who were playing various games. Some were dealing cards, others were twirling wheels with numbers on them, and some were playing games with chips. It didn't take Archie long to realise that he had been steered into a gambling den of the worst kind, and he was immediately on the alert for future developments. He watched every movement of his new friend, and noticed that he found it necessary to speak to several of those present in a low undertone. This didn't worry Archie, because he knew that he was in no danger except of losing money, and he felt that he could afford to lose some money, since he was sure to earn more by writing about the experience for the newspaper.

So he carefully observed all that was going on, making mental notes of the peculiarities of the place and the people. When at last the dark man came up and inquired if he wouldn't like a chance to earn some money easily, he very readily answered yes, and the man was overjoyed to find so willing a victim. Then, of course, Archie was introduced to the mysteries of the famous roulette wheel, of which he had read so much. Archie was interested in everything, and didn't mind losing four dollars in learning so much that was new. He succeeded in getting away when he had lost this sum, though the man assured him that he couldn't help winning back all he had lost, and much more, too, if he would but remain awhile longer. Archie was firm, however, and passed out into the narrow alleyways again, feeling that he had learned a great deal through a very small expenditure of money. He gradually found his way back into the crowded Surf Avenue, where there were hundreds of things, evidently, which he had not yet seen. The crowds, too, seemed greater even than before, and there seemed to be thousands of people arriving every hour from New York and Brooklyn, over the various street-car and railway lines, and by the excursion boats landing at the great iron pier. The noise was still deafening, and every one seemed to be having a splendid time in every way. "Surely," said Archie to himself, "no one can feel blue or despondent in such a place as this, where every one is full of fun, and apparently determined to have a good time while here." And he felt that he would like to remain longer, but he knew he should go back again to the city, so that he might see the editor, and tell him something about what he had seen and done.

So again he rode over the great Brooklyn bridge, and stopped on the other side at the handsome building of the Enterprise. It made Archie very happy to feel that he was now a reporter on such a great paper, and he found it hard to realise that so much good fortune had come to him in such a short time. He met reporters in the various hallways, and all of them spoke to him pleasantly, so that he began to feel that he had never been thrown with such pleasant men before.

He had no difficulty in seeing the editor this time, and found him a ready listener to the story of his Coney Island experiences. He insisted on Archie's describing all the men he had seen in the gambling den, and then asked him if he could identify them, if necessary, and also if he would be able to find the place again. Archie gave good descriptions of most of the men, and said that he could take any one to the place at any time. The editor lost himself in thought for a few minutes, and at the end of that time he rang for a copy-boy. "Ring for a messenger boy," he said, "and when he arrives come for a note which I want him to take to Mr. Pultzer's house." Archie stared with amazement at Mr. Jennings, and waited for further information. He wondered what was going to be done. He knew that Mr. Pultzer owned the newspaper, and he knew that it must be something important that Mr. Jennings wanted to write him about. He wasn't long left in the dark, and he felt very proud that Mr. Jennings should have confidence enough in him to tell him about his plans. "I think you have discovered something which will prove very important to the paper and the public," he said to Archie. "We have suspected for a long time that gambling dens have been flourishing in Coney Island, but up to now we have not been able to locate any of them. Now that you have found one, we hope to arouse public opinion to the danger there is in such places, and we hope to inspire a reform movement which will be strong enough to wipe them out entirely. I will hear from Mr. Pultzer in a short time, and then I want you to go down to the Island with some plain-clothes detectives and two other reporters. And I don't mind telling you now that there will be a good sum in it for you if you succeed in arresting any of the leaders of this gang. You can be excused for an hour now, if there's anything you want to do."

Full of enthusiasm over the coming adventure and his part in it, Archie hurried out to a quick-lunch counter and bought himself a light meal, for he feared that he would have to remain at Coney Island through the evening. Then, when he had finished, he returned to the newspaper office, where he spent some time in getting acquainted with some of the reporters who were working on the Morning Enterprise. He found them all very pleasant to meet, and he learned a great many helpful things from their conversation. The older men were able to give him many pointers concerning things that he should, and should not, do. While he was in the office of the Morning Enterprise Mr. Jennings came in, and, taking him along into the private room of the managing editor, introduced him to Mr. Van Bunting, who was the editorial head of the morning edition. Then Mr. Jennings told of the new scheme, and Mr. Van Bunting entered into it so thoroughly that before an hour three detectives, two reporters, and Archie were on their way to the Island.

Once arrived in the resort, which was as noisy and bright as in the afternoon, they all made a bee-line for the gambling den, headed by Archie, who surprised the others with his certainty and confidence as to which was the right direction. In a very few minutes they all stood in front of the dilapidated structure built out over tide-water, and Archie heard one of the detectives say that the place looked "mighty suspicious like." He gave three knocks just as the dark man had done in the afternoon, and in a few minutes the door was cautiously opened and a head made its appearance. The detectives lost no time in pushing their way in, amid great confusion and cries of fear, and it seemed only a few seconds until all the inmates were huddled in a corner, covered with pistols, and wailing in fear, when they weren't cursing through anger. Then they were all arrested and taken to the police station, where they were all refused bail, and placed in cells overnight. Then the reporters returned to the office of the Enterprise, where Archie was told by Mr. Van Bunting to write the story of his experience for the morning paper. This was his first work for the morning edition, and he took great pains to make his descriptions as complete as possible, and the details as accurate as he knew how to make them. And his hard work was rewarded by words of praise from the managing editor when he turned the copy in for editing.

Tired from his hard day's work, Archie then went up-town to the quiet square in which he had his home, and he was glad to get to bed. He had been nervous and excited all day, and found it difficult to sleep, but finally the tired eyelids lay quietly over the tired eyes, and Archie was dreaming of the cool and pleasant arbour of grapes at home, and of how the Hut Club was holding a special meeting there to devise ways and means of welcoming home their distinguished fellow member, Mr. Archie Dunn, who had achieved such great success in the city.

Notwithstanding his tired feeling, Archie was up early the next morning, and out at the corner to buy an Enterprise. He hastily turned the pages, trying to find the story of his Coney Island adventures, but he looked in vain. It wasn't visible anywhere. He was about to think that it had not been thought worth while printing when he noticed on the front page, in large letters, "The Boy Reporter's Great Discovery," and then followed the complete account, just as he had written it. This was the best thing yet. Just to think that his story had been considered important enough to print upon the front page! He could hardly believe it. Surely he had made great strides, and Archie began to realise that it is not experience that is most needed in journalism, but something to write about. "I have simply been fortunate

in finding some interesting things," he said, to himself, and then, after a light breakfast in a quaint Italian restaurant around the corner, he hurried down-town to the
office of the newspaper.

Archie was beginning to feel, by now, that he had worked for a long time upon
the paper, and as he had become acquainted with almost every one connected with
it, this wasn't a strange feeling for him to have. And it was evident, too, that the
editors intended to keep him busy for some time to come, and Archie realised that
he was in newspaper work to stay, for a time, at least. And he was overjoyed at the
prospect, for he found the whole business as fascinating and as interesting as he had
expected it would be.

Mr. Jennings, of the evening edition, was at the office when Archie arrived,
and sent for him to come in. "Here is fifty dollars," he said, "for your work of yesterday, and you will have more coming to you if these men are convicted. I want to
congratulate you on what you have done so far. Come in this afternoon, and I think
Mr. Van Bunting will have a new plan for you."

CHAPTER XII.

A SUCCESSFUL REPORTER--THE EDITOR DECIDES TO SEND HIM AS CORRESPONDENT   TO THE PHILIPPINES--LEAVING NEW YORK--IN CHICAGO.

AT three o'clock in the afternoon Archie was seated in Mr. Van Bunting's office, together with Mr. Jennings and several of the chief members of the editorial staffs of both editions of the paper. The editors had spread out before them, on the large table, several maps, and most of them were busily engaged in making notes on little paper pads. All the time, however, an excited conversation was being carried on, for some editors wanted Archie to proceed to the Philippines one way, and some thought that the better plan would be for him to go by some other route. But the important fact with Archie was that he was really going to be sent to the Philippines as a war correspondent, and that he was going to start very shortly. He had called on Mr. Van Bunting early in the afternoon, and had then learned for the first time what the new plan was to be. When the managing editor asked him how he would like to go to the Philippines, Archie could scarcely reply, so delighted was he with the brilliant prospect before him. He managed to stammer out a few words, though, in spite of his surprise. "I always thought war correspondents were selected from the most experienced men in journalism," he said, but Mr. Van Bunting only laughed. "That's what we have already done, my boy," he said, "and so far none of our distinguished correspondents have sent us a thing worth printing that we didn't already know. You see they can't send any more to us in the way of news than we can get from the War Department in Washington, and most of these men are too old fogy to send us anything out of the ordinary line of war correspondence. Now, what we want is for you to go over there and have some adventures, and write us something which will be different from what we have had before from the Philippines. We are sending you, because you have had no experience at such work, and will be sure to send us something unusual, and that is what we want. If you can only do as well in the tropics as you have done here in New York, we shall be more than satisfied with your work. I am sorry that I won't have time to give you very complete instructions, but perhaps it will be as well. And now some of the men are waiting outside to come in and talk this matter over, so we'll have them in now."

And Archie found himself in the midst of an editorial conference, during which many things were discussed. The meeting lasted more than two hours, and finally it was decided that Archie should travel from New York to San Francisco, and go from there to Manila on the army transport which was to sail on the twenty-fifth of the month. This meant that he would have to leave the city in two days' time, and Archie announced himself as quite willing to do this, as he had few preparations to make. The editors gave him many instructions about how he was to address his correspondence, and how he should proceed in the event of finding it necessary to send despatches by cable. And at the end of the conference he felt that he knew all that he would need to know, so that he could start off without fear of not being able to fulfil his mission. As far as Archie could understand it, his chief instructions as to duty were to the effect that he must have as many experiences as possible of as many different kinds, and that he must write about them in a perfectly natural way, just as if he were writing a letter to the folks at home. And he thought, of course, that this would be very easy to do.

Mr. Van Bunting gave him a letter of credit for six hundred dollars, which amount, he said, would probably be sufficient to pay his expenses while he was in the Philippines, and he also gave him a cheque for three hundred dollars, which was intended to pay the expense of getting to Manila. "Of course," said Mr. Van Bunting, "you can spend as much or as little of this as you please, and if you need more, and we find that the venture is paying us, why, we will send it on demand." Archie was so overcome with the knowledge that he possessed nine hundred dollars, that he could hardly thank the editor enough, and he made up his mind that he would spend as little as possible of the sum, and bring back part of it to Mr. Van Bunting upon his return. He couldn't imagine how it would be possible for him to spend so much money, and he felt that, after some of his experiences since he left home, he ought to be able to economise in many ways where other reporters wouldn't know how to save at all.

When the two days were up Archie had made all his preparation, and was ready to leave New York for Manila. He had sent a long letter home to his mother, telling her of his great good fortune, and enclosing a cheque for a hundred dollars, which she was to spend while he was gone. He told her that he would send her more money from time to time, and felt very proud as he mailed the letter. He told her, too, that if at any time she didn't hear from him on time, she could write to Mr. Van Bunting, and he would let her know of his whereabouts. This was something which Mr. Van Bunting had very thoughtfully advised him to do. "Your mother is sure to worry if the mails are overdue," he had said, "and if she writes to me, I will always be able to tell her of your whereabouts, for we can hear of you through our other correspondents, if not from your own despatches." So Archie felt that his mother shouldn't worry, since he was such a fortunate boy in so many ways.

The night before leaving he took a long farewell walk up Broadway. Everything was bright with light, and there was, as usual, a great crowd of pleasure-seekers on the sidewalks. It was all as fascinating as ever to Archie, and he felt sorry that he was to leave it so soon. New York had begun to grow on him, as it grows on any one living there for any length of time, who is in a position to appreciate the city's attractions. He felt that he would almost rather be on Broadway than in the Philippines, but of course he forgot this feeling when he remembered the confidence which Mr. Van Bunting had reposed in him by sending him upon such an important mission. So, after he had passed all the bright theatres and restaurants, he turned down a quiet side street and returned to his lodging, so that he might have a good night's rest before starting on his long journey.

At seven in the morning he was up again, and at nine o'clock he was bidding farewell to his many friends in the editorial rooms of the Evening Enterprise. Every one congratulated him upon his great good luck in getting such a chance to distinguish himself, and when they had done telling him that he had a great future before him, Archie felt happier than ever before in all his life.

The train left the Grand Central Station at one o'clock, and Mr. Jennings went with him to the station to see him well started upon the journey. "You may be sure we are all much interested in you, Archie," he said, as the train was leaving, "and we shall look forward anxiously to your safe return." These words made Archie very glad, for it cheered him to know that at least one of the editors liked him for himself as well as for what he could do.

The Southwestern Limited seemed to fairly fly along the banks of the beautiful Hudson, and everything was so delightful that Archie could scarcely believe that only a week or two before he had been walking along country roads, anxious to reach New York, that he might become an office boy. Every thing in this train was as perfect as modern ingenuity could make it, and there was no lack of interesting things to be examined, when Archie tired of the landscape. Then, when the train had been two hours out of New York, he discovered that the famous president of this great railway system was aboard, and, mustering up his courage, he determined to introduce himself. He had long been anxious to see this famous after-dinner orator and statesman, and here was a chance which might not come soon again. So he went back to the drawing-room, and found the great man to be quite as pleasant as he was interesting, and Archie was asked to seat himself and tell something about his experiences since leaving home. Everything he said was listened to with great interest, and this distinguished wit seemed to find many of the adventures very funny indeed. "You have certainly had some wonderful experiences," he said, when Archie had finished, "and I can appreciate your anxiety to leave school. I had that desire myself when I was a boy of about fifteen, but my father succeeded in making me change my opinion on the subject, and without much argument, unless you can call an ox-team and a stony pasture an argument. I had been asking to stay at home from school for a long time. I said that I was too old to be sitting there with a lot of girls and some younger boys, and that I wanted to work. Finally, my father said that I could stay at home if I cared to, and that he would let me work on the farm for a time. I was overjoyed, of course, at the prospect of staying out of school.

"The next morning I was awakened at four o'clock, and had to swallow my breakfast in a hurry, because I was late, my father said. Then he took me out to the barn and ordered me to hitch up the ox-team, and when this was done he took me out to a pasture lot and told me to pick up all the boulders there. Well, I picked up boulders all day long, and by evening my back and arms were so sore I could hardly move them. I was too tired to eat supper, and was soon asleep in bed. When my father awoke me at four the next morning, I told him to let me alone and that I was going back to school. After that I was content to stay in school, and said nothing more about leaving until I had finished the course and was ready to go to college."

And Archie thought it very queer that such a famous man should have had such experiences when a boy. He remained in the drawing-room for more than an hour, and when he left he felt perfectly sure that he had been talking with the most charming man in the world.

The train sped on and on, and when daylight came the next morning they were passing through Northern Ohio. Early in the afternoon they reached a great smoky metropolis, spread out for miles over the plains. Archie knew that this must be Chicago, and he decided, as this was Saturday, and the steamer wouldn't leave San Francisco until the next Friday, that he would have time to remain here over Sunday. So he left the train at the station in Pacific Avenue, and, Finding a hotel near the station, he started out to see something of the city famous for its dirt and for the World's Fair, two widely different things.

CHAPTER XIII.

SAN FRANCISCO--THE TRANSPORT GONE--WORKING HIS WAY TO HONOLULU BY   PEELING VEGETABLES ON A PACIFIC LINER--THE CAPITAL OF HAWAII.

ARCHIE found Chicago to be so widely different from New York that everything he saw was new and interesting to him. In the afternoon he managed to see something of the congested business section of the city, the tall office buildings, the great stores, and the famous Board of Trade. It was all very fine, he thought, but still it wasn't nearly so fascinating to him as New York had been on the first day he visited it. "Chicago seems so very much like some great town," he explained to the hotel clerk in the evening. "I feel as if I were not in a great city at all, because there are not the evidences of a large and wealthy population that we have everywhere in New York." Archie spoke of New York as if he had lived there always, and found much to criticise in Chicago. But toward evening he went up to Lincoln Park and the beautiful North Shore, and he felt that there was nothing more beautiful in New York than this magnificent park, and this handsome Lake Shore Drive, with its great houses whose lawns reached down almost to the lake itself. On the South Side of the city, too, he found some handsome streets and residences, but there was always that feeling of being in some rapidly growing town. It wasn't hard for Archie to realise that there were older houses in his native town than could be found anywhere in the great city of Chicago.

The greatest difference between Chicago and New York was to be noticed in the evening. Instead of the brilliantly lighted thoroughfares of upper Broadway and Twenty-third and Thirty-fourth Streets, he found but one street in Chicago which was at all illuminated, and the illuminations there were chiefly signs in front of dime museums. The streets, too, were not so crowded, and Archie almost longed that he could be back on Broadway, if only for a little while.

On Sunday he found Chicago to be a more noisy city than he had ever been in before on that day, and he found that the people made good use of their one weekly holiday. All places of amusement were open, and everything was running in "full blast."

The parks seemed to be very popular, indeed, and there were numerous water excursions upon Lake Michigan, to Milwaukee, St. Joe, and various other neighbouring cities. The street-cars were crowded all day long, many of them taking people to a Sunday game of baseball at the Athletic Park. All of this was very interesting and very new to Archie, but it didn't make him anxious to remain in Chicago any longer than Monday morning, so on that day he took the limited train for the Pacific Coast, for he had determined not to stop off again until he reached Denver.

Days of weary travel over a level, uninteresting stretch of ground followed the departure of the train from Chicago, and had not Archie found some interesting persons to talk with he would have been very weary long before reaching Denver. As it was, he managed to pass the time very pleasantly until the train entered Colorado, and after that he found much that was new to look at until he reached Denver. Here he remained for half a day, just long enough to see something of the city and a little of the neighbouring country. Then, taking a train for San Francisco, he reached that city on Thursday afternoon, and immediately began to make arrangements for sailing. He found, to his great disappointment, that the army transport had sailed the previous day, contrary to the expectations of the editors, and of the War Department itself, until the arrival of important despatches from Manila, which made it necessary to start the transport at once with supplies of ammunition. Archie hardly knew what to do. He had not anticipated anything like this, and could scarcely think of any plan for a time, but, finally, he proved himself equal to the emergency. He went to the naval agent and asked him when the transport would be due at Honolulu, and then he ascertained that a passenger steamer sailing for that port on Saturday would reach the destination three days sooner than the transport, so that by taking the liner he would have three extra days in Honolulu, and would be able to reach Manila on schedule time, after all. He at once decided that this was the thing for him to do, and as soon as he thought of taking the steamer it occurred to him that he might possibly be able to work his way to Honolulu, instead of paying the regular passenger fare, which he knew was high. So he went down to the great docks, and, after interviewing the second steward, he approached the chief steward himself, and asked if there wasn't something that he could do aboard the ship to earn his passage. The chief steward was thoughtful for a time, and finally said, "Well, yes, I believe there is. We haven't any one to peel vegetables yet, and if you think you care to do that work I guess we can fix you up all right." Archie didn't wait to consider whether peeling vegetables was hard work or not. He was too glad to have a position of any kind aboard ship to be particular about what his work was like, so he told the steward that he was willing to take the place. "Well, be on hand at about eight in the morning, and we'll see that you get to Honolulu."

Archie was overjoyed at his good management. "I am going to save about a hundred dollars," he said to himself, "and I will have this money to send home to mother." The rest of the afternoon and the evening he spent in going about San Francisco, and he found it to be more like New York than any city he had yet seen. There was the same cosmopolitan crowd on the main thoroughfares, and the same foreign districts here and there throughout the city. He found a great deal to interest him, especially at the Presidio, where everything connected with the army monopolised his attention. He made friends with many of the soldiers who were waiting to be sent to the Philippines, and hoped, on leaving, that he would meet some of them there, but he hardly expected that he would meet some of them in such a strange manner as it was his fate to do in Luzon.

After a good night's rest he was on hand early at the great steamer, where there was such a scene of bustle and confusion as he had never seen before, not even in New York. There was a throng of men with trucks who were loading the late freight, and there was a constant din of noisy voices, which, combined with the shrieks of escaping steam, made it impossible to carry on a conversation. Archie hurried aboard to find the steward, who immediately took him into the galley and introduced him to the cook, a large, fat Frenchman, with small, blue eyes set far back in his head. He seemed to be a pleasant man, and Archie thought that he would like him very much.

"Well, does ze youngster vant to vork, eh! Eef he do, I say you pare zis potate for dinee as quick you can." And the fellow pointed to a great bag of potatoes and a paring-knife. "Now you sit zere in da corner," continued the cook, "and keep out uf my vay." Archie found a stool and sat down, and, having brought an apron with him, he put it on and began work. The cook watched him closely, so that Archie soon learned to pare the potatoes very nicely, and of course he was able to get along faster and faster as he became more and more experienced. He managed, through great effort, to get the bag finished in time for dinner, or luncheon, as it was called on the bill of fare, and then he soon had to begin on other vegetables, which were to be served at the more complete evening meal. There were more potatoes, and some turnips and apples as well, to be prepared, and it kept the boy busy all the afternoon, cleaning as hard as he could, and never seeming to get done. The cook urged him always to hurry, and seemed determined to have everything ready on time. And Archie began to realise that he was working under a rather severe master.

He was again successful in getting the vegetables finished in time for the evening meal, and then he had an idea that he might be allowed to rest for awhile, but he soon realised his mistake. He was advised to begin work on the potatoes for breakfast if he didn't want to get up at two o'clock in the morning and pare them, so once more he took up the knife and began to clean and scrape. It was ten o'clock before he had finished, and he found himself too tired to spend any time on the after-deck with the crew, but went at once down into the small, stuffy room where he was to sleep with some of the stewards. His back ached from bending over, and his hands were all sore from being scraped.

Things were not very pleasant in this bedroom, but poor Archie was glad enough to be able to lie down on the hard straw tick and go to sleep. He slept soundly until he was awakened at four o'clock in the morning by the second cook, who ordered him up-stairs to work. There was no time to wash, and no place where he could wash, so the boy was obliged to go up just as he was, much as he disliked doing so. And once up-stairs there were various chores which were waiting for him in the galley, so that he was kept running until breakfast was served. And then it was time to begin paring vegetables again. This turned out to be the invariable daily programme, and Archie became rather discouraged. Had it not been for the thought that by doing this he was saving money to send home, he would have been miserable indeed, but this idea kept him hopeful. He was seasick, too, for a time, and was obliged to keep cleaning vegetables in the galley during the whole period of his suffering. The days when he was ill in this way were the most disagreeable ones of the voyage, and Archie often described afterward his feelings as he sat peeling potatoes with a bucket standing beside him. Each night he slept like a log, and each morning he was obliged to get up at four o'clock and start work again. It was the same thing day after day, tiresome and monotonous, so that Archie wasn't sorry when the beautiful island hove in sight, and they anchored in the picturesque bay of Honolulu.

Once at Honolulu, Archie's term of service on board the liner was over, and he was glad, indeed, to get ashore, where he learned that the transport had not yet arrived, but was expected in two or three days' time. These two or three days Archie determined to spend in sightseeing, and he spent his time to excellent advantage in visiting every quarter of Honolulu and seeing every side of life in the Hawaiian capital. He found it a delightful place. There was much that was interesting to see, the people were pleasant to meet, and the climate was perfect. He was almost sorry when he learned that the transport had anchored in the bay!

CHAPTER XIV.

THE VOYAGE ON THE TRANSPORT--A STORM AT SEA--ARRIVAL IN MANILA.

THE transport did not remain long at Honolulu, and before leaving Archie had several things which he wanted to do. In the first place, he felt that he ought to write the story of his experiences so far, and send it to Mr. Van Bunting; so he did sit down and describe in detail his experiences at cleaning vegetables on board the Pacific liner. He wasn't sure whether this was anything that Mr. Van Bunting would care to print, but he decided to send it on, anyhow. He would have been surprised had he observed the enthusiasm with which this letter was read in the Enterprise office a month later. He would have been no longer in any doubt as to whether it was anything worth printing had he read the Enterprise of the following day, when the letter appeared on the second page as one of the chief features of the paper.

Before leaving, too, Archie sent a long, cheerful letter home, saying nothing of his being seasick on board the liner, or of his having had to work so hard. He devoted his letter to telling of the many interesting things he had seen, and of his bright prospects for becoming a successful newspaper man. He wrote a shorter letter to Jack Sullivan, which was intended to be read to all the members of the Hut Club, for Archie felt that it was no more than right that they should know something of his success. He found it very hard to realise, away off here in Honolulu, that he had ever been a member of the club, and that he had ever lived in tents behind the barn. He felt very manly now, and his boyhood seemed far away behind him, so far away that he now felt like a man of twenty-five rather than like a boy of eighteen. He was beginning to realise that age is not always governed by years alone, but that experience does much to make one old.

As soon as the transport had anchored in the bay, Archie went aboard to present his credentials to the commanding officer. He found the general very pleasant to meet, and a very appreciative listener as he told of his scheme for overtaking the transport. The officer was surprised, of course, that such a young fellow should be going to the islands as correspondent, but the things he said were very encouraging to Archie, "I tell you what," the general remarked, at one time during the conversation, "I believe that a young fellow like Dunn, here, can find out a great many more interesting things than an older man could ever discover. You see the youngster has ambition and energy on his side, and ambition and energy are two mighty powerful things when they're combined. I'd hate to buck up against 'em myself." The other officers agreed with the general in this remark, and Archie began to feel that, after all, he might not have such a hard time finding interesting things to write about as he had expected.

The transport remained in port but one day, and in thirty hours after her arrival Archie found himself sailing again over the blue Pacific. The weather, for a few days, was almost perfect. A cloudless sky overhead, a warm breeze from the west, and a smooth sea made things very pleasant aboard ship, and Archie began to realise that there are times when it is delightful to be at sea. The vessel was very much overcrowded with troops, and the sleeping quarters were but little more pleasant than aboard the liner. Archie shared a stateroom with three sergeants, and they managed to have a lively time during the voyage. They played games, told stories, and slept in the afternoons, but all this, of course, grew rather tiresome after a time, and the voyage was becoming monotonous, when there came a severe storm which kept things moving for three days.

None of the navigating officers had expected a gale, so that when it came every one was taken wholly by surprise, and it came so suddenly that there was no time at all for preparation. The sky became quickly dark one afternoon about three o'clock, and soon the whole horizon was a mass of great black clouds, which every moment seemed to come lower and lower until they directly overhung the ship. There was great excitement aboard the ship. Officers hurried here and there shouting orders to their men, and the cavalrymen rushed about in a frenzy of haste, trying to devise means to save their horses, most of which were stabled upon the deck.

Archie looked on in breathless interest, and was surprised to find that he wasn't at all frightened. He even found himself making mental notes of the scene, so that he could send the story of it all to Mr. Van Bunting when he reached Manila.

There was but little time for rushing about, and it was soon evident that the horses would many of them be lost, because there seemed to be absolutely no way of saving them if the waves were high enough to break over the bulwarks. The storm soon broke in great fury, beginning with a fierce wind which swept the waves before it. There was but little rain, and the waves rose higher and higher with every minute, until the heavy ship began to roll and pitch in a frightful way, so that the soldiers began to think, some of them, that she would certainly sink. Finally the waves were so high they dashed themselves over the decks, and no one was allowed above the gangways. The cries of the poor horses, as they felt themselves being washed overboard, were frightful to hear, and many a trooper cried himself as he thought of his horse foundering in the raging sea without. Before many minutes all was as dark as night, though the watch pointed to but four o'clock, and all lights were burning below deck. It was impossible to keep a light above, for no lantern could burn in such a storm.

The waves began gradually to subside at ten o'clock at night, and a slow steady rain came, which soon calmed the sea to a great extent. As soon as it was safe to go above deck, it was found that more than a hundred horses had been lost overboard, and that one mast had been carried away. Down below nearly every man was in his bunk, for there was scarcely a person who was not seasick, and most of them wouldn't have cared if the ship had gone down with all aboard, such was their feeling of despondency. Archie was as sick as any of the others, but was able to make notes of occurrences just the same. And when he grew better the next day, he wrote an excellent account of the storm to send to the Enterprise on his arrival in Manila.

After this rough weather experience, every man aboard was anxious to reach port, and when, after many more days, the Bay of Cavite was reached, a great cheer went up from a thousand throats, for everyone was overjoyed at the sight of land.

The transport came to anchor off the forts which had once been Spain's, and it was announced that no one would be allowed to land for two days, until advices could be had from Manila and the interior of the island. This was very trying for

Archie, being obliged to sit on deck for two whole days, looking at a shore which seemed very inviting, in spite of the general dilapidated appearance of the various buildings and docks. Everything looked different from anything he had seen before, and the boy felt that he could hardly wait to be allowed to explore some of those streets which were so narrow, and those houses which were built in such a peculiar fashion.

Finally, the permission came for the troops to land, and Archie received the permission of the general to remain with them as long as he wanted to do so. And as he had no other plans, the young correspondent decided that it would be a good plan for him to stay right with one of these regiments, for the time being at any rate. He knew that they would be likely to be sent to the front immediately, and the front seemed the place for him to be.

And then he was already acquainted with many of the men, and with the colonel, and he realised that this would be an advantage to him in his work. So he made his plans to keep with them.

First they went to Manila, where they remained for a week. The quaint old city was a veritable fairy-land of wonders to Archie, who had never before been in a city so ancient, and here there were so many unusual things to be seen. There seemed to be absolutely no end to the winding streets, delightful old houses, and interesting churches, and the boy spent many days in exploring every corner of the island capital. The colonel warned him several times that he must look out for robbers and other suspicious characters, but Archie laughed at his fears. But the colonel was right, as he found later on.

CHAPTER XV.

ARCHIE STARTS OUT ON AN EXPLORING TOUR AND HAS SOME STRANGE ADVENTURES AMONG THE NATIVES--SEIZED BY THE REBELS.

THE days passed very quickly in Manila, the regiment was quartered in an old palace which had once been used as a residence by the Spanish governors of the islands, and Archie remained in the palace with them. There was very little to do while they were there. Each morning there were anxious inquiries for news from the front, but there was always the same discouraging reply that no trace had yet been found of the fleeing Aguinaldo. The men were gradually becoming disheartened at the long wait, and there were frequent statements by the officers that Aguinaldo would soon be caught if they were sent out after him. The dissatisfaction with the general in command grew stronger every day, and at last things reached a point where there was very little loyalty and patriotism displayed among the troops.

The drilling was continued, however, by order of the colonel, and every morning the troops marched out to a public square near the palace, and went through the same old manoeuvres which they had practised for months past. And it was harder for them to drill each week. At first they were willing enough to work, for there was then some prospect of their being able to use their knowledge in a fight, but now it was beginning to seem that they would simply remain in this old palace for a few months longer, and then go back again to San Francisco. With this opinion in their hearts, it is not to be wondered at that most of the men became slouchy and careless in their manners and dress, or that even the officers themselves became disgusted at the long wait for marching orders.

Things had been going on in this way for a long time, when Archie made up his mind that it was time he was hustling about and finding something to write about which would be interesting to readers of the Enterprise. He had sent two articles describing his life with the soldiers in the old palace, but he knew that he ought to find something more exciting, and more like his first articles. So, after much thought, he decided that a good plan would be for him to take a little trip into the interior of the island, to see whether he could find any traces of the insurgents. The colonel had held all along for a month, now, that the Filipinos were probably all about Manila, and still he couldn't get the permission of the general in command to go out and investigate the matter. The colonel figured that it would be an easy thing for the insurgents to come as near to the city as they cared to now, for Lawton and Wheeler were far away in the interior after Aguinaldo, and the troops in Manila were quietly drilling, and eating, and sleeping, with no thought of doing anything else. This line of argument seemed very reasonable to Archie, and he volunteered to go out and see if he could make any discoveries. The colonel assured him that he would be in no danger, even if he were caught by the rebels, for they would never suspect a boy of Archie's age and size of being a spy. So the lad felt no fear at all, and made what few preparations there were to be made before starting. He secured a knapsack from the commissary officer, and in this he placed what few belongings he wanted to take with him, together with his note-books and some provisions for the trip. Then he secured a small pistol, which he carried in his hip pocket, and he was disappointed because the colonel would not allow him to carry a rifle. And when he had everything ready he said good-bye to his friends in the regiment, and departed from the palace amid a multitude of cheers. At the last moment the colonel tried to dissuade him from starting, for fear he might meet with some accident, but Archie was determined to make the attempt.

It was his plan not to go farther than fifty miles in the interior, for he thought that if he found no traces of the rebels in that distance there would be little use in going farther into the forest, for, it would be almost impossible to find them there. So he set out gaily upon his trip of exploration, and Archie couldn't remember when he had been so happy before, save on that day when he first visited the office of the Enterprise. This adventure was exciting enough to please the wildest boy in America, and Archie could imagine how envious the other boys would be if they could but know the trip he was having. It had an official air to it, too, for had not the colonel been most anxious, in the beginning, that he should go, and did he not say that he would reward him handsomely if he were successful in locating any of the insurgents, or in proving that he had been right when he said they were near Manila? It was all as perfect an adventure as Archie could have imagined. He could not have planned a better one if he had been able to select any trip he could think of.

He planned that it would take him at least three days to walk fifty miles, and perhaps longer, for the roads were not very good in some places. He knew that he would find many villages and towns along the way, too, for the island was thinly settled in this neighbourhood. So if he were obliged to rest, he would never be at a loss for a place to get a bed. Archie couldn't help thinking, as he walked along the road outside Manila, this first morning, that he might find a body of the insurgents in possession of one of these towns. They were very bold, he had heard, and they probably knew that there were no American troops anywhere in the neighbourhood, outside the city of Manila itself. And, knowing this, he knew they wouldn't hesitate to camp at the very gates of the city, for they were marvellously successful in getting away into the interior whenever an American force made its appearance.

As he thought of this possibility, Archie couldn't help being a little fearful of what might happen to him should he fall into the hands of the insurgents, and he began to wonder if he had not been a little foolhardy, after all, in starting off on such a wild-goose chase. "But I will have something new to send Mr. Van Bunting about the interior towns," he said to himself, "and if I am captured, why, I will have a great deal to write about when I am released." This thought made the lad happy again, and he trudged along the road with as much vim and energy as he had displayed during those weary days when he was walking to New York to make his fortune. And it was a much more interesting country in which to walk than the New York State counties had been. The vegetation was rich and luxuriant everywhere, palm-trees, vines, and flowers growing in profusion all along the road. In every dooryard, in front of every hut, there grew what seemed to Archie a veritable fairy bower of the most richly coloured flowers in existence. And they were growing, apparently, without cultivation. He had seen nothing like them before, even in California, and he longed to pluck some of them to send home, if they had only been wax instead of nature's blossoms. As it was, he kept his arms filled with them for awhile, but after a time he grew tired carrying them, and was obliged to drop them by the roadside.

The country looked as if it might have been very prosperous at one time. There were plantations laid out in excellent fashion, and the soil seemed rich and fertile. But instead of growing crops, and storehouses filled with spices and coffee, there was desolation everywhere, and it was easy to see that the Spaniards had determined to leave but little behind them for the Yankees. Every other farmhouse and wayside hut was deserted, their occupants having gone, apparently, to join Aguinaldo, and the whole country, outside the towns, seemed to be wholly deserted and left to grow up in weeds and tangled vines.

The sun was warm, the sky was a perfect blue, and it seemed a delightful day in every way. But it made Archie sad to walk through a district which had been made so desolate, and he hadn't walked many hours before he wished that he might soon reach a town, where he could find some life, and where he could remain overnight. For by the middle of the afternoon he was tired walking, and made up his mind that fifteen miles was enough for any one to do in one day. But he was obliged to keep on walking for two hours longer before he reached a village, and the great sun was just sinking behind the blue hills in the distance when he entered the one main village street, which was long and narrow, winding in and out among the cabins and huts, as if it had been laid out after the houses were built, for the convenience of the people. It was a poor excuse for a public thoroughfare. There had probably been a pavement of some sort at one time, but now the street was a mass of rubbish of every sort, straw, dust, old bricks, and bits of stone being thrown together in every rut, so that it was exceedingly difficult to walk along with any comfort.

There was no life visible in the settlement. Almost every hut had its shades drawn at the windows, and there was absolutely no one to be seen in the street. As he passed down the road, Archie could catch occasional glimpses of black eyes staring at him through a lattice, or he could hear some muttered word as he walked close to a window. From these signs he knew that he was observed, and he felt very much embarrassed as he continued his walk down this deserted lane, for he felt instinctively now that hundreds of eyes were watching his every movement.

Finally, he came to the public square, and he sat down here to look about him.

From general appearances, he judged this to be a town of some two thousand inhabitants, for there was a very respectable administration building, and a good-sized church. There were but two streets of any consequence, the one by which he had entered the town, and another running at right angles in the opposite direction. In this latter street, as he stood in the square, he noticed a three-story structure with a sign outside, and he decided to go there and make inquiries as to where he might be able to secure a lodging for the night. It looked as if it might be an inn of some sort, or at least a store, so he walked rapidly up to the entrance and knocked twice upon the door. This place, in spite of its sign, looked more deserted and shut-up than any other building he had yet seen in the town, and he wondered whether he would receive any answer to his knocks. It was indeed a long time before he heard a sound within, but at last there was some muttering inside, the door flew open, and Archie found himself in the arms of three Filipinos, who threw him upon the floor and bound him, hands and feet. It was all so sudden that he had no time to cry out, and before he could say anything at all he was thrown into a dark room, and the door shut behind him.

CHAPTER XVI.

A PLEASANT CAPTOR--BRAVE BILL HICKSON ALLOWS AR-
CHIE TO ESCAPE--FIRST GLIMPSE OF AGUINALDO.

FOR a long time Archie lay still upon the floor, being unable to move a muscle from the shock of his encounter with the men, and because he was tightly bound with ropes. And then he at last went off to sleep, feeling frightened because he was in the hands of strange men, and a little satisfied, too, because he was the victim of some adventure which might turn out in a very interesting way.

When he awoke, it was morning, and the light came into the room through two small square windows, set high up in the wall. Archie looked about the room with great curiosity, but found little there to interest him. There was nothing to be seen but an old bed without spring or mattress, and a rickety chair with but three legs, which stood in one corner. The walls, he was surprised to observe, were hand-somely decorated with tapestries, and Archie at once made up his mind that this had at one time been a private dwelling-house, and had probably been owned by some rich Spaniard who kept a store on the ground floor, and lived in these rooms. The insurgents had probably driven the family out of the country and had taken possession of the house, which they had stripped of everything useful, leaving the tapestries and works of art behind them.

These suppositions were cut short by the entrance of a man who appeared to be a half-breed, and who immediately began to speak to Archie in broken English. The fellow had a pleasant face, and presented a fairly good appearance, and Archie wondered how he could have come to this place. "I suppose you have been won-dering," said the man, "why you have been thrown into this room, and it won't take me long to explain things. You see this town belongs to us just now, and we don't propose to have any Yankee spies around here to tell Otis of our whereabouts. There ain't no troops in this town now, but there's likely to be any minute, and we patriots was sent here to take possession of things and arrange quarters for our army. Let me tell you that the Filipino army will be in this town to-day, and if you don't look sharp you'll be the first prisoner to be shot. Aguinaldo isn't a man to deal easily with spies, and if he thought you was out here for that purpose he'd have you riddled with bullets in a minute." The man came up to Archie and began to undo the ropes. "I reckon I can trust you free for awhile, for there's no use in your trying to get away, with the Filipino army all around the town. Sit down there now, and I'll see that you get some breakfast. You can tell, perhaps, that I ain't no Filipino, nor never was one. I'm from Arizona, U. S. A., and I'm fightin' with these rebels for what there is in it just now. I'm mighty curious to find out how you come to be out in these diggin's, youngster."

Archie was willing enough to tell all about himself. He liked this man, in spite of his being with the rebels, and he felt that he would be able to make friends with him if he were careful to do so. And the best plan seemed to be for him to tell all about himself, how he happened to go to New York, and how he had been sent out here as a boy correspondent for the Enterprise. The man from Arizona listened to the recital with open mouth and eyes, and he frequently laughed outright at some of the experiences Archie described. When the narrative was finished, he seized Archie's hand, and said, "My name's Bill Hickson, and you can count on me after this fer a friend, youngster. I'll swan if I ever heard tell of sich nerve in my life. I'll see that you get out of this scrape all right, but you must be careful to keep up appearances of being under guard. I'm a big-bug in this Filipino shack, but I wouldn't dare to let you out openly. So you jist kind of lay around and look despondent, and depend on me to make things as easy for you as I can. You kin come down-stairs now, if you like, and I'll present you to my friends. There don't none of 'em speak no English but me, and all I can do is to interduce you, and tell 'em that you ain't no spy, and that you are very sorry you ever ran up agin this here town. And I guess I'll be expressin' your sentiments exactly, won't I?" Archie nodded, but in his heart he felt that he wasn't sorry he had run up against the town. This Bill Hickson, in himself, was a character worth going miles to meet, and if what he said was true,

Archie stood a good chance of seeing the notorious Aguinaldo, with his army of Filipinos, before the day was over.

When he reached the lower floor, he found several men lounging about in another poorly furnished room, and they were all similar in appearance to the men he had seen at the door the night before. They looked at him in an indifferent way, and didn't seem surprised that he should be walking about without restraint. Bill Hickson stepped up to some of them, and, after a few words in some language Archie didn't understand, motioned for the boy to step up. He was told to shake hands with "all the gents," and after he had done so he was offered a cigar, and Archie began to realise that it was a very good thing that he had a friend at the Filipino court. He thought, too, that if these men were samples, Aguinaldo had a very poor lot of retainers, and later on he perceived the real cause for the failure of the rebels to do anything more than keep up a constant retreat. It was plain to see that the followers of the rebel leader were "in it for what it was worth." They had no difficulty, any of them, in getting enough to eat, and often they had opportunities to enjoy themselves in great fashion by taking possession of some Filipino village and ejecting the inmates of some particularly fine house, with a well-stocked wine-cellar.

In looking out of the window Archie perceived that the town looked very different this morning than when he saw it the evening before. Instead of drawn blinds and shuttered windows, there was everywhere an evident attempt at decoration in honour of the coming army. The streets were crowded with a throng in holiday garb, and some of the soldiers of the rebel army had already arrived, as they could be easily distinguished by their ragged dress and ridiculous airs, walking up and down the street. It was all such a scene as Archie had never seen before, and would have made a great success as the scenario for a comic opera. But as a welcome to an army, supposedly victorious, it was a dismal failure, and Archie wondered what General Aguinaldo would think when he entered the town and saw such shoddy patriotism everywhere. He hadn't long to wait, however, before seeing the famous rebel and the effect upon him of the celebration in his honour. It was about ten o'clock in the morning when he rode into the public square, followed by about two hundred ragged Filipinos, armed with all sorts of guns and pistols. Archie saw the arrival from the roof of the building which was his mock prison, and he could scarcely refrain from laughing outright when he saw the boasted Filipino "army." It was the poorest excuse for a body of troops that he could imagine.

Aguinaldo rode a fine bay horse, as did several of his followers, but by far the majority of the regiment, if such it could be called, was afoot, and most of them were barefooted, too. The rebel leader looked very much like most of his pictures, with the exception that he had an older look, and some gray hairs about the temples. He was attired in a gaudy uniform of some sort, with epaulets and a Spanish general's hat, and he carried himself with great dignity of manner. Dismounting from his horse, he entered the administration building, where he held a conference with the town officials, and probably made them pay over whatever money was in the treasury "for the cause." He remained within for two hours or more, and all this time Archie stood upon the roof and watched the remarkable scene in the streets below. The troops had scattered, and were engaged in robbing the housewives of whatever they had in their houses to eat. And the women seemed willing to provide them with whatever they could afford, and there was much enthusiasm evident everywhere. But the celebration was very quiet, in spite of the friendly reception, There were no bands of music, no cheering, and no singing of battle-hymns. The whole affair reminded Archie of some camp of a section of the famous Coxey army, when he had seen it long ago. The soldiers were no better dressed than tramps, and there was but little more discipline among them.

And the celebration and occupation of the town came to a sudden end. While Archie stood upon the roof at noontime, he saw a runner enter the administration building in great haste, and in a minute Aguinaldo came hurrying down the steps. Then there was a great commotion in the streets, and the two hundred followers of the chief were seen assembled in the square, and before they were all there the general was riding out of the town toward the interior of the island. There was no noise, and the inhabitants stood about apparently speechless, and wondering what had happened. Their reception had come to an untimely end, and their hero had left them unceremoniously. Soon the last of the straggling troops were out of the town, and just as Archie was beginning to think of going down from the roof Bill Hickson stuck his head up and gave him some astonishing news. "Stay where you're at, young feller, till these fool Filipinos gits away from here. You saw how they skedaddled, didn't ye? Well, Uncle Sam is comin' after 'em with shot-guns, and old Aggy heard the news just in time. He is bound for the jungle, about forty miles southeast, and he won't reach it until to-morrow night, anyhow, and if the officers are quick they may be able to catch him. Now you stay here, lad, and give 'em the news when they git here. They'll thank you for it, and you may be the means of gittin' this fool of an Aguinaldo captured. If you does, why, your future's all right. And ye can tell the colonel, or whoever's in command, that Bill Hickson is still with 'em, and that he's doin' his best fer Uncle Sam, and tell 'em that Aggy has got about three thousand troops altogether, but only about a thousand with him. Now, good-bye, lad, and I hope I'll see ye again."

And Archie saw brave Bill Hickson get down from the roof. He brushed some tears from his eyes as he realised that here was a brave soldier doing good work for his country. A moment later he saw him running across the square with four of the Filipinos, and waving his hat to the "youngster" as he went. He followed him with his eyes as long as he could, and then he sat down and made a solemn vow that Bill Hickson should be named among the heroes of the war.

CHAPTER XVII.

ARRIVAL OF THE AMERICAN TROOPS--ARCHIE THE HERO
OF THE REGIMENT.

ARCHIE descended from the roof, and found everything below in a state of wild disorder. The fleeing rebels had taken with them all they had time to get together, but in their haste they had left behind many of their most useful belongings. In a cupboard of the dining-room Archie found a supply of food and wines sufficient to feed several people for a week, so he supposed that it had been the intention of the occupants of the house to remain for some days. The news that the Americans were coming upset all their plans, however, and now, as often before, they were obliged to flee before them, leaving behind most of their creature comforts in the way of food and furniture.

"What a life they must be leading," thought Archie to himself, "going from one place to another, constantly endeavouring to hide from the Americans. Now in some town, now in the wilderness, and again venturing as near as possible to the boundaries of Manila." And he could scarcely help admiring their courage, or recklessness, rather, in camping so near the head of the American government, where they might expect to be caught in a trap at any moment. But Archie realised, too, that such an army can get away in a very short time, and he began to have serious doubts as to whether the Americans would ever be able to capture Aguinaldo and his men. For knowing the islands perfectly, and being able to get from one point to another in the easiest and quickest way, the rebels have a great deal in their favour.

Selecting some canned beef and some native bread and cheese, Archie managed to make a very good meal for himself, though he ate hurriedly for fear some of the rebels might return. As soon as he had finished he returned to his position on the roof, for there he knew that he would be safe in case the building was entered by the townspeople. From his high perch he looked down into the streets, and was surprised to find them as quiet and as much deserted as they had been the night before. The news of the coming of the Americans had been effective in quieting the enthusiasm of the morning, and all the townsfolk had again entered their homes and put the shutters up before their windows. One would have taken the place for a deserted village, judging from appearances. But Archie knew that within the shuttered windows and barred doors there were hundreds of people waiting anxiously for the arrival of the American troops, and making ready to come out, when required to do so, and again declare their allegiance to the stars and stripes. The cowardly wretches were diplomatic enough to be always on the side of the victorious. When the rebels occupied the town they were loyal to them, and when the Americans came, as they often did, they came out into the square and cheered loudly for Uncle Sam. But of course the Americans knew very well that their sympathies were with the rebels, and the rebels knew it, too, or they would never have dared to venture so near Manila.

About five in the afternoon, there was a sound of many men marching along the road, and in a little while Archie was able to see the Americans coming down the street. It was a sight to cheer his heart after all his experiences of the last day and night. The column was marching at double-quick, and the handsome colonel rode a great gray horse at the head of the regiment. Archie saw that they would reach the square in two or three minutes, and, throwing discretion to the winds, he descended from the roof, almost fell down the stairways in his haste, and was soon running toward the administration building. He mounted the great steps leading up to the portico, just as the colonel rode into the square, and the expression of surprise on the faces of all the men was funny to see. In a minute every hat was off, and the regiment was giving "three cheers for the boy reporter," while the colonel, rapidly dismounting, hurried up to speak with Archie.

"Why, how did you come here?" he demanded. "Haven't the rebels been here, and how did you escape them? Which way did they go, and was Aguinaldo with them? For pity's sake, say something."

Archie wasn't long explaining things, and his news was so explicit and so valuable that the colonel grasped his hand and said, almost with tears in his eyes, "God bless you, lad. You may have aided us to catch the gang, and anyhow you've proved your bravery."

By this time the regiment was standing at ease, and all the men were watching Archie and the colonel with great interest. Knowing that they were all curious to learn how the lad happened to have escaped the rebels, the good colonel made a short speech in which he explained everything. He dwelt particularly upon the bravery of Bill Hickson, and held him up as a model for all the men to follow. "And now three cheers for Bill Hickson and our boy reporter again," he cried, when he had finished, and they were given with a will by all the men.

The regimental officers held a short consultation, and it was decided, on the strength of the news brought by Archie, to push on after the rebels as fast as was possible. But it was now sunset, and there was no use trying to go farther to-night, so it was agreed that the best plan would be to give the men a good rest overnight, as they had made the entire march from Manila since five o'clock in the morning. "They will do all the better to-morrow for the rest," said the colonel. Archie was valuable in being able to guide the officers to the building where he had been confined, assuring them that they would find everything needful there in the way of food, and a place to sleep. Some of the soldiers were quartered in various houses of the town, for the people had soon turned out into the street again, and had expressed their friendship for their "masters," as they called them. Archie could hardly refrain from laughing as he saw some of those who in the morning had bowed down to Aguinaldo vowing everlasting allegiance to our flag, and he assured the colonel that he couldn't be too careful while in the town to guard against surprises. "No one knows the beasts better than I do," was the answer. "I know they can't be trusted."

Archie was invited to remain in the building with the officers, and while they prepared and ate a lunch he busied himself in writing a description of his last two days' experiences. He knew that a messenger would soon start for Manila, and that a boat would leave that city on the next day for Hong Kong, so he wanted to get his narrative written in order to send it to Mr. Van Bunting at once. He felt that he had some very interesting things to write about, for it wasn't every correspondent who had seen Aguinaldo, and had been captured by the rebel army. He knew that most of them were content to remain in Manila, and send only what they could get from the general in command, and that this description of the rebels would be something new, at any rate. So he wrote it very carefully, and succeeded in getting it ready in time to send, so that it would be in the office of the Enterprise in less than a month. As he sat at the table writing, Archie thought of the great changes which can take place in one's surroundings in a few weeks. It seemed ages to him since the day when he left home for the first time, and the experiences he had on his way to New York seemed now to belong to the far-away period of his boyhood. He was beginning to feel very old now, because he had been through so much of late, and he could hardly realise that he was still eighteen.

He wrote a short note to his mother at home, telling her not to worry, and assuring her that he was in good health and in no danger whatever of being captured by the rebels, for Archie felt quite safe after his experience with the insurgent leaders. He knew that no one of their prisoners was ever likely to come to a very bad end. They were far too slipshod in their methods of holding prisoners. He was sorry not to be able to send a longer letter home, but he knew that this note was much better than sending nothing at all, and that it would make his mother very happy to hear from him at all.

The officers, when Archie returned to the dining-room, if such it could be called, were engaged in making a very good meal from the provisions in the cupboard, and they thanked Archie warmly for leading them to such a good place. "By Jove," said one of the captains, "we sha'n't want to return to Manila at all, when we can get such grub as this is outside." But the colonel assured them all that they needn't expect to find such accommodations everywhere in the interior of the country. "No doubt we'll all be living on plantains in a day or two, if we don't catch that fox of an Aguinaldo. And I'm willin' to bet now that we won't find him. That feller's too slick for us. He's proved it many a time before."

"And to think that he was here only this morning! The nerve of him, to come within twenty-five miles of Manila!" said another.

"I'll be mighty well satisfied if we can catch a few of his ragged men," continued the colonel. "That will be something to have accomplished, anyhow, and more than some other regiments have done, when they were sent after him. He's the cutest feller I've heard of in a long while. If it wasn't for Bill Hickson we'd never hear tell of him, even. He could enter Manila, I believe, and go out again without us ever knowin' it at all."

Archie was now called on to tell something of the rebel leader's appearance, and how he had acted while in the town.

"I didn't see very much of him," said Archie, "because he spent most of the morning with the big-bugs of the town, over in the administration building. But when he rode into town on his horse he looked mighty dignified, though he fell some in my estimation when I saw him standing up. He looked rather dumpy then. He carried himself with a lot of dignity, a little more than was becoming, I thought, and he received the cheers of the people as a matter of course, and hardly took the trouble to acknowledge them, even by a bow. The officers of the town treated him with great deference, and I guess there's no doubt but what the Filipinos look upon him as their leader."

"Oh, there's no doubt of that," said the colonel. "We've learned that long ago. They stand up for him whenever he needs them, and they give him all they've got to help carry on the war."

The meal finished, the officers smoked awhile, and then went to bed, for they were to be up at four in the morning.

CHAPTER XVIII.

THE MARCH AFTER THE REBELS--THE FIRST BATTLE--AR-
CHIE WOUNDED.

ARCHIE was awakened at four the next morning by the sound of the bu-
gle, and, hastily dressing, he hurried down-stairs to learn the plans of the
officers. He found that they were going to start on the march as soon as
the men had drunk their morning coffee, and Archie immediately made
preparations to go with them. The colonel looked on in amazement. "Why are you
packing your knapsack!" he asked. "You surely don't think you're going with us?
You never in the world can stand this hard march in the hot sun."

"Oh, yes, I think I can," said Archie. "You see I have walked a great deal in
these last two months, and I don't think I will have any difficulty in keeping up
with the troops. And I do so want to see some fighting, and to learn whether you
capture Aguinaldo. You don't object to my going, now, do you?"

"No," said the colonel. "If you think you can stand the marching, and are so
anxious to come, why, I suppose you can do so. But you mustn't blame me if anything should happen to you."

Archie was ready enough to promise this, for he had no idea that he would
meet with an accident of any kind, and so he continued to pack his things in the
knapsack. The rebels had emptied everything in a corner, and had evidently intended taking the knapsack with them when they went; but they left so hurriedly
they couldn't possibly think of everything, and so had left it behind, much to Archie's relief, for he would have been unable to secure another one anywhere outside Manila. In a very short time the regiment gathered in the streets immediately
about the square, and soon the men were marching out of the town, much to the

gratification of the residents, who watched them from their roofs and windows. Archie fell in at the head of the column, and found no difficulty in keeping up with the soldiers near him, though they were marching at a rapid rate.

The town limits were soon passed, and they swung into the white country road, which presented the same scene of desolation which had been everywhere visible to Archie on his way from Manila. The farm-houses were nearly all deserted, and there was but little attempt at cultivating the soil, which would have been productive enough had it not been overgrown with tangled vines and weeds. And as they went farther into the country the wilderness increased, until at last the road itself was filled with growing vines, and the men had difficulty in walking. Every little while some trooper would fall headlong, tripped by some vine, and the others would laughingly help him up before passing on. These little incidents did much to enliven the march, which became monotonous after the first six or seven hours, and Archie appreciated the mishaps very much until he took a few tumbles himself. He was usually, much to the amusement of the officers, marching at the very head of the regiment, and "setting the pace," he said, so that he was more likely to trip than any of the others. He was always the first to discover a snake in the road, too, and kept a great stick with which to kill them. He seemed to have no fear of them, but walked up to lay them out, and on one occasion the colonel warned him just in time or he would certainly have been bitten by a snake whose bite is certain death. This experience made him more careful, but he still kept his place at the head of the regiment, and came to be called the mascot by the men.

At noon the regiment halted at a grassy spot, where there were trees, and made their dinners from their knapsacks. The officers warned them to go carefully, or they would find themselves without provisions before returning to Manila, for they had been so sure of catching the rebels at the town behind that they had neglected to bring along many supplies. Now, of course, they didn't know how long it would take them to find them,--two days at least, and probably longer.

Archie had stocked his knapsack with some food from the old headquarters in the town, so that he felt safe for a few days, at any rate. He ate carefully, however, and was careful not to waste anything, for he realised that he might be called upon to aid some of the soldiers before long.

Dinner over, the regiment marched on again, for the officers now began to think that they had made a mistake in not pursuing the fleeing rebels the night before. They met several Spaniards, who told them that Aguinaldo had marched all night long without stopping, so that he was now at least thirty-six hours ahead of them, and some of the men began to be discouraged, saying that it was no use following him up with such a small force. "Other regiments have tried to find him in this way, and none of them have succeeded," said one of the privates to Archie. "They keep us marching for three or four days, and finally they decide to return to Manila, without having found any trace of the rascal beyond hearing that he had passed this way or that."

The officers couldn't depend upon what the natives told them of Aguinaldo's movements, for, almost without exception, they were in his favour, and always lied to the Americans to try to throw them off the track. It was due to this that they proceeded very cautiously, and still, notwithstanding their extreme care, they found themselves, when night came on this first day, in a small village where no one had seen anything of the rebel army. There was no denying the fact that they were off the trail, and the colonel stormed about in a terrible way when he learned of their mistake. There was no use going back in the dark to hunt for a trail they had mistaken in the daylight, so the regiment remained in the village overnight. They were a lot of very discouraged men, and the officers were enraged at the mistake, for which there was no one but themselves to blame.

Early in the morning they retraced their way, and started off in an opposite direction to the one taken yesterday. It seemed that this must certainly be the path taken by the rebels, but the regiment marched until nearly noon without seeing any signs of them. Then, when they had halted for dinner, the colonel decided to let the men rest while two companies were sent ahead to reconnoitre, and report as to whether there were any signs of men having passed this way. He was beginning to think that the whole affair would be a wild-goose chase, and he decided that, if these companies found nothing, the whole regiment would return to Manila forthwith, probably to be the laughing-stock of the army there.

The remaining companies had nothing to do now but lay about on the soft grass, and rest. They were encamped in a stretch of grassy loam in the midst of what appeared to be a dense forest, and all about were evidences of the great fertility of the soil. The vegetation was so dense that one could scarcely see through it, and the glade was cool and pleasant, though overhead the sun was shining as warm as ever. It was a lovely oasis in a wilderness of undergrowth, and the men enjoyed it to the utmost.

About three in the afternoon the sound of firing was heard in the distance. First there was one shot, then another, and several more at rapid intervals. Archie was one of the first to jump to his feet, but in a second every man was at attention, with his musket in his hands. The colonel listened closely for two minutes, and then the firing began once more, and this time it seemed nearer. He hesitated no longer, but gave the order to march ahead. "They've evidently found the cowards at last," he muttered to Archie. "You stay here, where you will be out of danger." But Archie was determined to do nothing of the kind. He felt his pistol safe in his hip pocket, and when the companies swung out of the forest and into the road he was marching in his old place at the head of the column. Again the colonel ordered him to remain behind, but Archie insisted that he would not, "Then go to the rear," cried the colonel, angry for the moment. "I will not have you shot down by a rebel sharpshooter the very first one." And Archie knew that he would have to obey.

The column went ahead at double-quick, and finally broke into a steady run. Every minute the noise of rifle-shots sounded nearer, and it seemed probable that the two companies were retreating before the insurgents. The men were wild to reach the scene of the firing, and the officers had all they could do to keep them in line. All the time they were running hardly a sound was heard save the noise of their boots upon the soft earth, and they all knew that they could probably take the insurgents by surprise.

Archie's heart was beating very hard as they drew nearer and nearer to the scene. He felt that he was about to see his first fighting, and he determined not to miss any part of it. So he gradually ran ahead until finally he was almost at the head of the column again.

The troops made so little noise that the two companies, retreating slowly, were upon them without knowing it. But when they discovered that their comrades had come to their aid they set up such a cheering as Archie had never heard before, and immediately faced about and went ahead again. The rebels were about a quarter of a mile behind, marching rapidly forward, and firing as they came. Some of them were running among the trees at the roadside, firing incessantly, and hitting some poor soldier almost every time they fired. They were the famous sharpshooters, of whom the soldiers in Manila had heard so much.

When the rebels observed that the Americans had received reinforcements, they halted suddenly, and before they could turn about the Yankees were almost upon them, firing volleys into them as they came. Many of the insurgents fell in the roadway, and the others fled wildly in every direction. Most of them entered the dense forest, where the Americans captured nearly a hundred of them after the others had surrendered, and some were such good runners that they escaped down the roadway. The whole rebel army presented a scene of wild confusion. Some of the men knelt and begged for mercy, and some cried out in a horrible way as they saw the dreaded Yankees advancing. But it was all over very soon. The prisoners were placed in line, and marched back along the road, and the dead, of which there were about fifty, were soon buried. Aguinaldo had escaped in the forest, and no one suggested that he should be followed. All the officers knew that such a course would be useless, and most of them were very well satisfied with what had already been accomplished. The prisoners numbered more than six hundred, and the dead a hundred more, while there were about seventy-five wounded. So if what Bill Hickson said were true, not more than two hundred insurgents could have escaped.

Among the seriously wounded was a man whom Archie recognised immediately as one of his captors of two days previous, and while he was looking over the bodies for the other men, he came suddenly to brave Bill Hickson, lying face downward in the road. He almost screamed with fear that he might be dead, and when one of the men hurried up to him he told him who the man was. The colonel was soon on hand, and it was found that the brave spy was not seriously wounded, and would recover soon under proper treatment.

When the insurgent wounded were cared for, it was discovered that the two companies sent out to reconnoitre had also suffered losses, and when they marched back along the line of their retreat no less than five dead and about twenty wounded were found. This sad news threw a gloom over the entire regiment, and when they started back to Manila they marched in quiet, and without rejoicing over their victory, which had proved so costly.

Poor Archie, when they started to march, found, to his great disgust, that he was so weak he couldn't walk far, and he thought this must be due to the fright he had received. He was very angry with himself, until the surgeon examined him and announced that he had a bullet in his arm. And then Archie confessed that he had felt a stinging sensation at one time during the firing, but had thought nothing of it. Now his disgust was turned to great delight, for the idea of being wounded in battle was glorious to his mind. "I'll bet I wounded more than one insurgent," he told the surgeon, "for I discharged every barrel of my revolver." The wound was not at all serious, but he was told to be quiet for a few days. He was given one of the rebel horses to ride back to Manila, and he felt like a real hero in many ways.

CHAPTER XIX.

RETURN TO MANILA--IN THE HOSPITAL--CONGRATULAT-
ED BY ALL--WRITING TO THE PAPER OF HIS EXPERIENCES.

IT took the regiment much longer to march back to Manila than it had taken it to follow the rebels, for the wounded of both sides had to be carried, and the arrangements for carrying them were very imperfect. Fortunately, most of them were able to ride horses, and the officers were successful in securing wagons enough to carry most of the others, but there were about a dozen who could neither ride horses or lie in wagons, but had to be carried on stretchers all the time. Of course this was slow work, and the officers were glad enough when they reached the town with the three-story building. Here they found things very much as they had left them, two days before, save that the inhabitants were more abject than ever to them, now that they had captured most of the rebel force.

It wasn't an easy matter to find quarters for so many men, and some of the Filipinos were obliged to camp in the public square overnight, while the wounded and ill were given beds in the various houses of the town. The inhabitants were required to furnish food, too, for the Americans were entirely out of almost everything. They still had some hardtack, but of meat and coffee there was none. The people of the town pretended to be very glad to serve their "masters," but every one knew that the natives would be only too glad of a chance to cut the throat of every Yankee soldier.

The officers again occupied the old building which they had used during their former stay, and Archie was invited to share it with them, for they expected to rest in this town over the next day, before proceeding to Manila. The men's uniforms and equipment generally needed cleaning and repairing, and the colonel was anxious for them all to appear as well as possible when they returned victorious to the island capital. So the next day was spent in cleaning and washing, and by evening most of the soldiers looked as if they had never left Manila. Then came a surprise for every one, for into the town marched a regiment of militia from Manila, sent out to see whether the first regiment needed reinforcements. They set up a great cheer when they learned that most of the rebel force had been captured, and the night was spent in a celebration of the great event. A band was scraped up in the town, the great hall of the administration building was thrown open, and there was dancing and music until an early hour in the morning. All the belles of the town turned out to welcome the soldiers, hypocrites that they were, and they danced with their enemies as readily as they would waltz with their own dear Filipinos. Every one seemed to have a good time, and the soldiers went to bed just in time to get three hours' sleep before starting for Manila in the morning.

It was a great sight to see the two regiments, with the prisoners, march out of the town at five the next morning. They made a fine appearance in their well-brushed uniforms and bright equipment. The townsfolk watched them out of sight, and then most likely cursed them for a lot of vagabonds, but the soldiers didn't mind their curses. They were all very happy at the prospect of getting back to Manila again, and no one was more glad than Archie. He had somewhat recovered from his wound now, and rode in his old place at the head of the column, where he was the centre of interest to every one. The men congratulated him on having proved such an excellent mascot, and he laughed and talked with them until he was tired.

The outskirts of the city were reached about five in the afternoon, and as they marched through the streets to headquarters a band of music preceded them, playing popular and patriotic airs. The sidewalks were crowded with people, and Archie felt happier than for a long time, because every one was curious to know who that boy could be riding at the head of the troops, alongside the colonel. He was known to most of the other troops in Manila, and received many a cheer from them as they saw his arm in a sling, and when they finally reached the general's headquarters, he was honoured with a handshake and the congratulations of the commander himself. This was the climax to a very happy day, and Archie went to bed in his little old bunk feeling that he was a very lucky boy for having been wounded in battle.

Of course the next few days were very busy ones for all the men, and for Archie, too. He was obliged to tell, over and over, the story of his experiences, and how he had managed to escape from the rebels when they had him. This story always made the men roar with laughter, and increased their already strong contempt for the Filipino army. He told, too, about brave Bill Hickson, and that gentleman's cot was always the centre of an admiring throng of visitors, who shook his hand and told him how proud they were of what he had accomplished. And all the poor hero could do was to smile feebly, for he was still too ill to talk much.

Archie felt that he had almost volumes to write about his experiences in battle, and he did send a very long account of this encounter to Mr. Van Bunting. It was written in his boyish way, but one of the officers who read it said that it was the best thing of its kind he had ever read, so he wasn't at all backward about mailing it. All the other newspaper correspondents in Manila were wishing they had gone with the regiment and witnessed the battle, but they had stayed in Manila, thinking that this would be like the other expeditions of the kind, a mere wild-goose chase, which wouldn't amount to anything at all. They were all very anxious to get the details of the affair from Archie, but he was shrewd enough not to tell them anything of value. And the other correspondent of the Enterprise in Manila insisted that Archie should send a cable message describing the affair, as well as a written account, and this he finally consented to do. The correspondent added a long account of Archie's personal bravery, how he had been wounded, and how he had ridden back to Manila at the head of the column. Archie would have been very much embarrassed had he known this, for he was still modest, but the first thing he knew of it was from a letter he received a few weeks later from Mr. Van Bunting, congratulating him on what he had accomplished, and telling him that he had long since more than earned his six hundred dollars. But for weeks he was ignorant that any one in New York knew of his being wounded.

The days now began to pass as before in the camp at Manila. The wound in Archie's arm was healing slowly, but he was hardly able to use that member for a month or six weeks. Bill Hickson did not fare so well. He lay for weeks on his cot in the hospital building, and was hardly strong enough, for awhile, to talk. He was improving slowly, but the doctors said it might be two months before he was able to walk about and take his former active part in the campaign against the insurgents. This enforced quiet was very trying to the brave man, and Archie spent many hours reading to him, and telling of various things he had learned at school and elsewhere. This constant companionship served to strengthen their already close friendship, and it was soon known among all the troops that Bill Hickson and the boy reporter were inseparable. And every one who knew the story of their experiences looked upon them as the two chief heroes of the war so far, because as yet there had been few feats of bravery in the desultory campaigning against the rebels. General Funston had swum the river, of course, but many held that not even that feat compared with the bravery of Bill Hickson in serving as a spy under Aguinaldo's very nose. The more people heard about his experiences, the more remarkable they thought him to be, until at last he was by far the most popular man in the army at Manila.

Archie sent many interesting letters to Mr. Van Bunting, telling of the adventures of the brave spy, and one day he received a cablegram telling him to send at least one of these letters by every steamer, for people had become interested in hearing about him. So for some time Archie wrote about Bill Hickson rather than about himself, and was glad of the opportunity to do so. He knew that if a letter were published every week or two in the Enterprise Bill Hickson would soon be famous, and this was something he was very anxious to accomplish. He felt that no fame could be too great for such a man, and no praise too strong.

The commanding general decided, about this time, to begin a more active campaign against the insurgents. It was now the month of December, and with the beginning of the new year he wanted to inaugurate a series of attacks against them in every part of the islands. He was beginning to feel the criticisms of the papers at home, and of the newspaper men at Manila, and he felt that something must be done immediately to retrieve his lost reputation for active fighting. Every one, as soon as this announcement was made, wondered what plan would be pursued to worry the rebels into submission, for it was now generally agreed that the Americans would hardly be able to capture the whole rebel army. It was too evident that they were familiar with numerous hiding-places in the islands. The only thing to do seemed to be to prevent their getting supplies, and to drive them from one point to another, hoping that they would become discouraged in the end and submit to the inevitable.

So far the campaigning had consisted chiefly of such expeditions as that accompanied by Archie, and most of these had returned to Manila without having even seen a rebel soldier. It was not surprising, then, that the general was becoming discouraged, and that he was anxious to try a new policy.

No one knew what the new plan would be until one day several cruisers and gunboats made their appearance in the harbour. There had been no war-ships at Manila for several weeks, and every one was surprised that so many should arrive at once. There were rumours of a German onslaught, and also gossip saying that Japan had decided to interfere, but all these were set at naught when the general announced that the war-ships were to be sent around the islands to bombard the rebel villages, and to drive the rebel troops to the interior of the islands, where it would be hard for them to receive supplies.

This news made Archie very happy, and a plan at once occurred to him. Why shouldn't he and Bill Hickson be allowed aboard a cruiser? It would be the best thing possible for their health, and he set about getting the necessary permit from the admiral.

Bill Hickson was able to be about now, and he was overjoyed when Archie said he thought they could arrange to go. "I'd like nothing better than a voyage in the good salt air. I believe it will do me more good than a month in the hospital," he said. Archie secured a very strong letter from the general, and one day he stepped aboard the flag-ship in the harbour. He had no difficulty in seeing the admiral, and found him to be a very pleasant man to talk with. He read the letter carefully, and then shook Archie cordially by the hand. "Yes," he said, "I've heard of you, and of your friend, too. Every one in Hong Kong knows how you two together bearded old Aguinaldo in his den, and robbed him of most of his troops. It did me good to read about it in the New York papers, too, and to know that you are both getting your just measure of credit for the achievement."

Archie blushed, and assured the admiral that he didn't do very much, that it was all owing to Bill Hickson's bravery. "Oh, yes, I know," laughed the admiral, "you lay it to him, and he will most likely give you the credit. I've seen your kind before. But I like you all the better for your modesty, lad. Of course you and your friend can have a berth aboard ship, and aboard the flag-ship, too, where I can see you both very often. You can come aboard whenever you wish, and stay as long as you like."

Archie could hardly thank the good officer for his kindness, and hurried back to Manila. He found Bill Hickson waiting for him at the wharf, and they rejoiced together over the good news.

CHAPTER XX.

AROUND THE ISLAND ON A WAR-SHIP--BOMBARDING A FILIPINO TOWN.

IT was early one morning that Bill Hickson and Archie went aboard the flag-ship, but all hands were on duty there, and the gallant cruiser was raising anchor preparatory to sailing off on her errand of pacification by means of shell and shot, The two newcomers were assigned a pleasant stateroom where they would not be far from the cabin of the admiral himself, and where they could step out of their door upon the quarter-deck, and get all the fresh air they needed. It was a very comfortable place, with two soft bunks, and every convenience usually found aboard the fastest ocean liner. When the fellows saw it first, they could hardly believe it could all be for them, but the officer assured them that it had been given them by the admiral's own orders. So there was nothing for them to do but accept the kindness, and to settle themselves down to having just as pleasant a time as possible during the coming weeks at sea.

It was generally understood that the cruiser was to make a complete tour around the island of Luzon, investigating every suspicious port, and shelling towns when such action proved necessary to convince the rebels of Uncle Sam's superiority. The voyage was expected to occupy nearly a month, for there was no reason for them to hurry, and the admiral said he would like to take things easy.

Neither Hickson nor Archie had ever before been aboard a war-ship, and they both found much to interest them during the first few days at sea. Every movement of the crew, every action of the ship, was of great moment to them, and they found no lack of entertainment in examining the great guns and the equipment of the vessel in the way of firearms and ammunition. Archie became much interested, too, in the science of navigation, and spent much time with the captain on the bridge, or with the pilot in the lookout, learning as much as possible about how the movement of the vessel is controlled. Before long he had mastered the rudiments of the art, and the captain told him that he might some day make an excellent navigator if he continued to take as much interest in the charts as he did now. And Archie told him that he was determined to master as much as possible of the business during the voyage. Before he returned to Manila he knew more about it all than even the captain would believe he knew, and the knowledge was very valuable to him in days to come.

The two visitors aboard took their meals at the officers' table, and they kept the whole party interested for many days, with their stories of the war in Luzon and of their very unusual adventures both at home and in the Philippines. For it turned out that Bill Hickson had visited almost every part of the United States, and had lived in all sorts of places. He had been a cowboy in Texas, and a miner in the Klondike, and he had also been a policeman in Chicago. He knew more stories to tell than any other man at the table could think of, and he told them in a way that was wholly charming.

Archie found that every one was very much interested in hearing about his leaving home, and how he had happened to become a reporter on the New York Enterprise. No one seemed to tire of listening to his stories of his adventures in the great American city, and many of the officers told him that they would give a good deal to have had his experiences in life.

And so it wasn't long until the two chums were friendly with all on board, and after awhile things went along as though Archie and Bill had never lived elsewhere than aboard ship. There was nothing exciting for nearly a week. The cruiser steamed slowly along the shore, sometimes stopping entirely, while the officers levelled their glasses upon the beach, to see whether there were any signs of the rebels being there. Sometimes, if things looked suspicious, parties were sent ashore to reconnoitre, but they seldom returned with news that would encourage the admiral to investigate further. The days passed quietly, and the two convalescents enjoyed themselves well enough. They were both much improved already by the trip, and felt almost as well as ever. They each had a steamer chair, and hour after hour they sat upon the deck and watched the ever-changing panorama of the tropical shore. Now the beach would descend slowly to the sea, and there would be numerous palm-trees and luxuriant vegetation growing close within view, but again there would be steep clips, which looked menacing to a ship in the dark. But it was all beautiful, cliffs or sandy beach, and Archie thought he had seldom passed such a wholly delightful week.

But, of course, it all became monotonous in time, and every one, even the officers, longed for a change. The reconnoitring parties were sent out more frequently now, and every one hoped each time that they would return with news of the rebels, but they were always disappointed. The admiral now determined to steam ahead more rapidly, so that they might get around the western end of the island. It was evident that there were no insurgents along this shore, and as there were no villages of any consequence, either, he was anxious to reach the southern shore, where it was known the rebels had recently been gathering. The towns, too, were very numerous here on account of the excellent fishing, and it was hoped that some good work might be accomplished for Uncle Sam before another week passed.

Subsequent events soon proved the wisdom of the admiral's plan. The cruiser, it seemed, had no sooner rounded the western point than signs were visible of rebel activity ashore. It was one Tuesday morning that a village was sighted, built around a narrow inlet of the sea. When the binoculars were levelled upon this harmless-appearing settlement, it was soon perceived by the admiral that there were soldiers in the streets with the rebel uniform, and that the insurgent flag was flying from the administration building in the village square. All this was just what had been expected, and there was great rejoicing aboard the cruiser. Every man, without exception, almost, was anxious to be one of a party to be sent ashore to attack the rebels, but the admiral hesitated before sending any one at all. "It is impossible to tell from here," he said, "how numerous the rebels are, and it is quite possible that they may have a large force of men in the village. If the appearance of the streets is any sign, there must be quite a force of them in the place." But every one laughed at the very idea of there being a rebel company of any consequence in the place, and the admiral was finally prevailed upon to send a boat ashore, armed with thirty men.

"Remember," he said, "if you come to grief, that I advised against this venture. Don't be too bold, or risk too much, for though I can shell the place, that won't help you any, once you are captives."

But every one was anxious to be one of the party in the boat, and the officers had a hard time making selections. "You can go, Archie, because you're a correspondent," said the captain, "and you can go, Mr. Hickson, because you're a brave man," and then he continued to pick out men until the required number was secured. Of course there were many disappointed ones left aboard the cruiser, but the captain assured them that they might have their chance yet.

The boat was soon off, and it was noticed that there was great excitement ashore as soon as the departure was observed. All the inhabitants, it seemed, were gathered upon the beach, anxiously awaiting developments. They seemed to be absolutely ignorant of what the presence of a war-ship in their harbour meant, and were apparently not at all anxious as to the outcome of this visit. One of the men told Archie that they had probably never seen a war-ship before, and that they wouldn't know a cannon at all. "But we'll let them know the meaning of our presence," declared the sailor, "if they shoot at us." The boat drew every minute nearer the shore, and it was soon perceived that there were many soldiers among the crowd on the beach. Every one thought it remarkable that they should be so quiet, but not one of the natives made a move until the boat was within two hundred feet of the shore. Then one of the rebel soldiers suddenly raised his rifle and fired at the boat. The lieutenant in command stood up in the boat and gave the order to return the fire, and a perfect volley of shot was poured into the crowd, which immediately scattered in every direction. The rebel soldiers, however, seemed determined to stand their ground, and they were so numerous, and kept up such a steady fire, that it was deemed best to return to the cruiser, which was signalling for this action on their part. So the boat was turned about as quickly as possible, and the sailors pulled for the cruiser, amid the derisive yells of the Filipinos, who had gathered again upon the beach. The rebel soldiers continued their firing, but were such poor marksmen that but three of their shots took effect. One sailor was shot in the arm, another in the side, and still another was shot in the leg as he stood up to take aim at the rebels. None of these wounds, it was afterward discovered, were at all serious, though they were enough to arouse the anger of the entire crew.

When the boat reached the cruiser again, preparations were at once begun for bombarding the town. The natives still stood upon the shore, and it could be seen that they were immensely proud of their present victory. It was amusing, then, to see the change in their behaviour when the great six-inch gun of the cruiser belched forth a cloud of fire and smoke, and a burning shell landed in the village street, apparently just in front of the administration building, which was soon afire. The poor natives fled in every direction, and the rebel soldiers followed their noble example, and took to their heels, too. Another shell followed the first, and soon several buildings were burning in the village. The admiral watched developments carefully, and finally he decided that they would be glad to surrender the village if another boat was sent ashore.

Accordingly, the same boat started out again, with three new men in place of those who were wounded, and for sake of effect the cruiser steamed farther in toward shore. This time there were no crowds upon the beach, and the thirty men marched to the burning buildings, where the natives fell before them, begging for mercy. The soldiers were nowhere to be seen, so the crew took possession of the town and slept there, in company with thirty more sailors, that night.

CHAPTER XXI.

IT may go without saying that the sixty men from the cruiser had a very interesting time before the night was over. The entire village was in a constant uproar; the poor natives, horrified by what they had witnessed during the afternoon, ran hither and thither, some even leaving the place entirely and starting for the interior with their goods and families. The rebel soldiers had evidently gone for good, and a small party sent out to look for traces of them returned without learning anything of their whereabouts. The bombardment of the village had certainly had great effect.

It was only a tiny place, with possibly not more than a thousand inhabitants, but there were evidences that it had been formerly a flourishing town. There were fine residences in some of the streets, which were now quite deserted, and there were some very respectable business houses in the village square. All these had once been occupied by Spanish traders, who had been driven away when the rebels came, and if the insurgents had never come the town might now have been a booming place. But the rebels were lazy, as usual, and did no work, so that now the fine residences were vacant, and the business blocks stood empty.

Some of the sailors looked about for a casino, where they might be able to find entertainment of some kind for the evening, but every place of amusement was closed, and the streets were deserted. Since the occurrences of the afternoon all the people had locked themselves into their houses, to await the departure of the Americans. But, even though the casino was closed, the Yankees managed to have a good time. They sang and danced and played the banjo until an early hour in the morning, when they finally went to sleep, leaving only two for a night watch, for there was no danger that the insurgents would return, after their engagement, in which they had lost six men.

When morning came, some officers landed from the cruiser, and all the villagers were summoned to the public square and made to swear allegiance to the American flag.

In the afternoon the cruiser steamed away again on her errand of forcible pacification, and more days of quiet watchfulness followed, as the vessel steamed along near the shore. There were many small villages along this coast, but all of them seemed peaceful and free of insurgents. The captain even said that some of the people in them probably didn't know that there had ever been a war between Spain and the United States. Archie, who had enjoyed his experiences during the occupation of the last village, now began to be impatient again at the long quiet. The day when the cruiser bombarded the administration building would be a memorable one to him, and the succeeding events were just such as he had been longing to see for months. And then to think that he had taken part in the occupation of the village. It was all very wonderful, but very real, too, and for several days he took much pains in writing an article for the paper describing the events leading up to and including the capture of the village. And in the narration Bill Hickson was an important character. He had again proved himself a hero of the first water by insisting that the boat proceed when the first attempt was made to land, and by being the first man ashore when a landing was finally effected. He was a leader in everything that was done. He marched at the head of the squad when they marched through the streets of the village, calling all the people to assemble in the public square, and he stood beside the officers with his rifle handy when the ceremony of swearing allegiance was gone through with. When it was all over he was called to the admiral's cabin aboard the cruiser and congratulated for being so brave and so ever-ready to lead in any dangerous undertaking; but Bill Hickson simply blushed and said he hadn't done "anything worth mentionin'." The men aboard thought differently, however, and he was even a greater hero after this adventure than he had been before.

Archie, too, received the congratulations of the admiral. "You have been a brave boy," he said, "and deserve much credit for showing so little fear in the face of danger. I hope you will be rewarded upon your return to New York for your bravery while with us here." Archie, too, blushed, and said that he had no doubt that Mr. Van Bunting would treat him fairly when he reached New York again.

And Archie was now beginning to wish that the time for his return would soon arrive. It was the month of February, and he had been away from America an age, it seemed to him. He felt that he had seen most of what there was to be seen in the Philippines, and when this naval tour was over with, the active campaigning would no doubt cease until the rainy season was over. So for many reasons the boy wished he might be able to start home soon, and as the days passed he became more and more anxious to receive word from the Enterprise that he might return. He had sent many interesting articles to the paper, and would be able to write many more just as interesting upon his return, so he felt that the editors wouldn't object to his early return.

For an entire week the cruiser found no signs of the rebels, but at last there came a day when they were steaming slowly along near the shore, and saw, back among the trees, some specks of white resembling tents in shape. Immediately the whole vessel was excited, and there was much gossip and wonder as to what the tents could be doing there. The admiral at last decided to send two boats ashore to investigate, and gave strict orders that the men should be cautious and not allow themselves to be ambushed or caught in a trap of any kind. Of course Archie and Bill Hickson were among the crew of the first boat, and each was as fully armed as any of the sailors.

The two boats pulled quietly for the shore, keeping close together, and they were beached at the same time. The natives, or whoever occupied the tents, had evidently not yet discovered them, and the men halted upon landing to decide what they had better do. The tents could be plainly seen through the trees, and there was smoke rising from a fire somewhere in the neighbourhood, but there were no noises which could be heard so far away. It was decided to march up to the tents and find out who occupied them, and the column kept close together as they advanced, for things were so quiet it was feared the rebels, if such they were, might be in ambush.

The men got within a hundred feet of the camp, when they heard several terrible yells in succession, and several natives ran out from behind one of the tents, screaming at the top of their voices, and not pausing to look around at all. The officer in command of the company of men was much disturbed by this demonstration, and, without pausing a moment, gave the order to fire. Five of the natives fell immediately, but the other six kept running, and soon disappeared among the trees on the other side of the clearing. The men stood still awaiting developments, but though they waited several minutes nothing more was heard, and it was decided that the camp must be deserted. So they marched up to the tents, and then the officer almost fainted, for inside the first one he entered was standing an American flag, and scattered about were the accoutrements and camp equipment belonging to an American force in the field. There was now no doubt but what the tents belonged to an American regiment, and that the fleeing natives were either servants or prisoners, more likely the former. The men were all much excited at this discovery, and the officer ordered the natives to be looked after at once. It was found, however, that all but one were dead, and he expired within an hour, so that the men felt that they had killed five innocent men, a thought which made some of them weep, hardened though they were.

It was now decided to await the return of the regiment, which was out, the officer thought, on a practice march, and could not possibly be gone much longer. So the men lounged about on the grass for more than an hour. Then, about three in the afternoon, a rifle-shot was heard in the near distance, and instantly every man was on his feet, rifle in hand. "They must have found the rebels," said the officer; "so be ready, men, to help them out, should they be retreating to the camp." This supposition turned out to be correct, for a few minutes later some members of the regiment came running into camp and announced that a large body of insurgents was after them. Later the remainder of the regiment followed, and the joy of the colonel when he found these unexpected reinforcements was very great. "There must be more than fifteen hundred rebels," he said, "and they will all be on us here in less than an hour, for their sharpshooters have been following us up for a long time. I was beginning to think that we would be unable to fight them, for they seem to be well equipped, but with the cruiser to kelp us we can whip them at once. The thing to do will be to let them come on without suspecting that we have received any help, and then, when the fight is getting a little warm, or they are about to charge us, let the cruiser fire a few shells into the air, and it will all be over. Most of them are country troops, and have never seen a cruiser, so they will be too much frightened to speak when they hear the thunder of the guns, and see the shells explode in the air. And then they have a village about three miles back from the coast, and if you can send a few shells into that village it will simply ruin the insurgents.

"I had no idea of meeting these rebels," the colonel then explained. "I took the men out for a little practice marching, but before we had gone far we encountered these sharpshooters, and later discovered that they had all these men about a mile and a half away. Then we decided to return to camp as quickly as possible, to get more ammunition, and we felt, too, that we would stand a better chance of resisting them here among the trees. But now we will soon finish them up, if you will just send a man out to tell the admiral of our plans." Archie immediately volunteered to carry the information, and as he could be spared better than one of the soldiers or sailors, he was permitted to undertake the mission. So he started out, and was on board the cruiser in a very short time. The admiral was dumbfounded to learn that American troops were encamped on the shore, and in imminent danger of being defeated, and he at once set about giving orders with great vigour. "We will show them how they can attack a small regiment of Americans with their ridiculous army," he declared, and at once gave orders for the vessel to move inshore. "But wait," he cried, a minute later, "I see by my chart that there is a deep stream about a mile up the coast, and if I am not mistaken we can enter this stream and perhaps get very near the advancing rebels. We may even be able to destroy them before they have a chance at our soldiers," and the old admiral almost danced in the enthusiasm of this idea. So the cruiser steamed rapidly up the coast, and was soon at the mouth of the stream, which seemed to be the estuary of some great river. Then she steamed up-stream, and, sure enough, the admiral soon discovered the rebels marching rapidly along the road, about half a mile away. They had evidently not perceived the cruiser, on account of the high reeds growing along the banks, and the admiral gave orders to begin firing.

The first shell rose high in the air and exploded with a deafening thunder, and when the smoke cleared away it was seen that the insurgents were almost paralysed with fright, and had just discovered the cruiser in the river. But this first shell had not hurt any one, and another was immediately ignited. This one exploded over the very heads of the troops, and many of them must have been killed. Those who were not either killed or wounded turned about and began to run, and their leaders were powerless to make them stand their ground. One shell followed another from the cruiser, and hundreds must have been killed outright among the insurgents. Finally they were all running, and it was soon perceived that the Americans had advanced, and were now pursuing them with great energy. So the cruiser could fire no more shells, and the admiral ordered her about and back to the anchorage onshore.

It would take many pages to describe in detail the events of the remainder of that afternoon, as Archie witnessed them from the deck of the cruiser, and learned of them later from Bill Hickson. The insurgents were nearly all killed or taken prisoners, and it was found that they numbered nearly two thousand. So it was a great achievement to have vanquished them all. The affair turned out to have been the greatest victory of the war, so far.

CHAPTER XXII.

RETURN TO HEADQUARTERS--A LETTER FROM THE EDI-
TOR, WITH PERMISSION TO RETURN TO NEW YORK--BILL HICK-
SON GOES, TOO.

ARCHIE left the cruiser when she was once more at anchor, and, going ashore to the American camp, he found things in a very lively condition at the close of the afternoon's battle. Every man was very jubilant over the retreat which had been turned into a great victory, and Archie was congratulated on having been the lucky man to carry the news of the coming of the rebels to the admiral. The officers were all in the best of humour, except the colonel, who felt somewhat sad on account of the death of his five faithful servants, as the men first shot turned out to have been.

"There were never any better men than they," said the colonel, "and I would almost as soon my own men had been shot." But he bore the ship's company no malice for their mistake, which he said was a very natural one.

After the capture of so many rebels, and the killing of so many others, it was felt that the rebel army in this part of the island was pretty well disbanded, and that it would soon disappear altogether. It had been known, from the very beginning of hostilities, that there was a large force of insurgents somewhere in this neighbourhood, but not until to-day had the colonel seen anything of them. But it was impossible, all the officers said, that there could be any more troops about, for these two thousand represented a very considerable portion of the entire rebel army. And now that these were done away with, the colonel said there was no need of his remaining any longer in this place, and that he would like to get back to Manila as quickly as possible. Hearing this, the admiral said he thought room could be made for all the men aboard the cruiser, and that they could all return at once if they so desired. This generous offer was at once accepted by the colonel, and the next day the work of embarkation began. By night every man was aboard, and a place of some kind had been found where he could sleep, but of course, every portion of the vessel was much overcrowded. This only made things all the more lively, however, and Archie, as well as all the others, thought he had never enjoyed any trip so much as these three days spent in getting back again to Manila. There was always fun of some sort going on. If some one wasn't dancing, there was sure to be singing. And then there were several ingenious games which were invented for the occasion, so that time never passed slowly. Indeed, there were many who were sorry when the capital was finally reached, but Archie was not among these, for he expected some mail to be awaiting him from the editor of the Enterprise. And he hoped that in this mail he would find permission to return to New York.

All officials were very much surprised when the cruiser anchored off Cavite, but the admiral explained that he thought it no use to spend more time in touring the island, even though the month which it was supposed to take him had not yet expired. He said that he felt sure there were no more insurgent villages along the coast, because it was perfectly evident, from all signs, that the rebels were all in one division. And this division, of course, had been vanquished four days previously.

When the report of the engagement went the rounds there was much enthusiasm, for it was felt that at last some progress was being made against the insurgents. The admiral was a popular hero at once, and Archie, with Bill Hickson, was again the centre of admiration and interest in the old palace, where they both returned.

Archie was surprised to find no mail awaiting him, but he was not discouraged, and wrote two long articles to send to the Enterprise. One described the great engagement, and the other was descriptive of the daily life aboard ship upon the return to Manila. These articles, with the others he had written during the latter part of the cruise, were sent off at once, and Archie felt confident that they would be read with great interest by Mr. Van Bunting. And now the days passed very pleasantly in Manila. He had a great deal to tell his comrades in the old regiment, for none of them had been out of Manila since he left, and were very anxious indeed to hear about the events of the round-the-island tour. And Archie was very willing to tell them all he could, for he had been much interested in the entire voyage, and never tired of talking about it.

Still, while things were very pleasant, and he was having a good time in many ways, Archie was very anxious to see New York again and to get back to America. And then, what was even more important with him, was the knowledge that he would certainly be allowed to visit his mother upon his return. Therefore he was a very happy boy when he one day received two letters from the Enterprise office, one from Mr. Van Bunting, and one from Mr. Jennings. They were both very encouraging and very friendly. Mr. Van Bunting wrote to tell Archie how delighted they all had been with his success in finding interesting things to write about, and he enclosed a check for three hundred dollars, which he thought "would come in handy now." The letter from Mr. Jennings was of later date, and stated that he had prevailed upon Mr. Van Bunting to allow Archie to return to New York, to work upon the Evening Enterprise. It was a very delightful letter, Archie thought. "We believe," wrote Mr. Jennings, "that we can use you here to very good advantage, and we will be glad to have you return as soon as possible. I enclose two hundred dollars to pay your expenses home again."

So now it was all settled that Archie was to leave Manila for New York, and, now that it was sure he was going, he felt somewhat reluctant to leave the soldiers with whom he had become friendly, and to get away from all this life of adventure which had been so interesting and so delightful in many ways. It was hard, too, to leave the dear old palace in Manila, through which he had wandered so often, and every room of which had for him some story of a Spanish prince or a great governor-general, wealthy and wise. There would be none of all this at home or in New York, but then there would be something better; there would be mother, and the old grape arbour, and the Hut Club.

On investigation, Archie found that the quickest way to get home would be to travel by way of Hong Kong and Yokohama, taking the steamer from there to San Francisco. It would take him more than a month to make the trip, and, as it was now the second week in March, he could hardly expect to reach New York before the first of May. He at once cabled Mr. Jennings that he would leave at once for Hong Kong, and received an answer telling him to do so by all means, and to continue to write letters describing his trip. Archie knew that these letters would probably not reach New York any sooner than he would, but he did write them, anyhow, and he did see some of them appear in the paper after his arrival.

Archie was overjoyed to learn one day that Bill Hickson had received permission from the commanding general to return to the United States, and he at once hunted up the bashful hero, and insisted that he leave at once, and make the trip with him. This was finally agreed to, and when it was settled that the two old chums were to travel homeward together the whole camp in Manila was interested in the news. They were both very popular, and almost every night before their departure there was a pleasure party of some kind arranged for them. One night they would give a regular "stag," as they called them, and then again they would arrange a sort of musicale, at which there would be clog-dancing, banjo music, and various games to increase the fun.

The four days passed very quickly indeed, and at last the day for sailing arrived. There was a great throng at the pier to see them off, and there was no end of good wishes and stories of the good times now gone by. When the steamer finally moved out into the open, there were three cheers each for Archie and "brave Bill Hickson," in which every man appeared to join with all his heart and voice. And there were tears in Archie's eyes at having to part from such true friends. It was hard to tell, too, when he would ever see any of them again. He realised that hereafter his path and theirs would probably lie in different directions. He was going to New York to work as a reporter, and they, if they were not killed in battle, would be scattered in all parts of the great United States, at the mustering out of the troops. It was all very sad, and even Bill Hickson seemed to feel the solemnity of the occasion, for he had nothing to say for many hours after the vessel had started on its journey.

Archie, too, felt homesick at having to leave, and they went to bed very early, apparently feeling that the best thing under such circumstances was to be asleep. And when morning came they both felt somewhat better, for Archie arose filled with hope for the future, and more anxious than ever to reach home. Bill Hickson, too, was not loath to return to the United States, even though he had no relatives waiting there to welcome him. The poor fellow had been through a great deal while in the Philippines, and his constitution was almost wrecked by the constant strain to which he was subjected. He had never fully recovered from his accident of several weeks before, and he felt that he needed a rest from the constant excitement and worry of life in the army. He was tired, too, of being a spy. He had never relished the work, but he had realised how necessary it was for the Americans to have some one to follow up Aguinaldo and let the general know of his movements. "They'll be a long time catching him now," he said, time and again, to Archie. "He's a much shrewder man than they think, and he knows his Philippine Islands like a book. He can go from one place to another without the Americans ever knowing where he disappeared to, and without some one to follow him they will never be able to learn anything of his movements."

Bill had received nearly two hundred dollars in back pay, so he felt quite rich, and Archie told him that if he should happen to run out, and need more money, he would be very glad to furnish it to him, For Archie was now determined to take Bill Hickson to New York, and introduce him to Mr. Van Bunting, feeling sure that the wise editor would thank him for bringing to his attention a man at once so interesting and so worthy as this hero of the war had proved himself to be. But for the present Bill would discuss nothing of the kind. He was thoroughly content to sit beside Archie on the warm steamer deck, and watch the ever varied surface of the Indian Ocean.

CHAPTER XXIII.

HONG KONG--A HAPPY TIME IN TOKIO--HONOLULU AGAIN--ARRIVAL IN SAN FRANCISCO, AND A GREAT RECEPTION BY THE PRESS--ARCHIE AND BILL ARRIVE IN NEW YORK, AND ARE THE HEROES OF THE HOUR.

AFTER a short and pleasant voyage they reached Hong Kong, and Archie found this city to be much more interesting than he had expected to find it. It was charming, he thought, to run across a place which combined the conveniences of England and America with the picturesque oddities of China and Japan, and he enjoyed himself to the utmost during the two days they spent there. Bill Hickson enjoyed the place, too, and they would both have liked to remain longer had it been possible for them to do so, but they were anxious to see something of Japan before sailing for San Francisco, and their steamer was due to leave Yokohama in eleven days.

But they did enjoy Hong Kong to the utmost while they were there. They called first, of course, upon the American consul, whom they found to be an exceedingly pleasant man. They learned, to their great surprise, that he had read of Archie Dunn, and of Bill Hickson, too, in the Enterprise, and Archie began to think that his paper had a much wider circulation than even the editors claimed for it. He thought it very remarkable, at first, that a man living in Hong Kong should have read about his Philippine experiences in a New York paper, but of course, after he thought of it awhile, it didn't seem such a very remarkable thing, after all. And after this, when they heard of people having read of them, they weren't so much surprised, having come to realise the tremendous circulation of this paper.

The consul did all in his power to make their stay in Hong Kong pleasant. He was anxious to have a formal dinner for them, but Bill Hickson said that he would much prefer not having to dress up, and Archie was willing for Bill's sake to forego the honour. So they spent their two days in going about the city, visiting the quaint Chinese shops, and seeing everything of particular interest. They found many wonderful things to look at, and Archie said that he couldn't imagine any more delightful place; but Bill told him to wait until they reached Japan, for he'd find that much more charming than Hong Kong. "I've been there before," said Bill, "and I know what I'm talkin' about, and I say there ain't no such place on earth as Japan for interestin' things to look at, and pleasant things to do." And when, a few days later, Archie was initiated into some of the mysteries of Japanese life by his experienced friend, he was willing to admit the truth of all he had heard concerning the land of the chrysanthemum. He found everything quite beyond his expectations. The people themselves were more quaint in their dress and manners than he had expected to find them, and the houses and the pagodas were much more picturesque than he had imagined they would be. And the whole atmosphere of the country seemed filled with romance and history, and it wasn't at all hard to believe that the Japanese have longer family trees than any other nation on earth.

They spent a few days travelling through the provincial districts of the little kingdom, and then they reached Tokio, where Bill was anxious to spend several days. "I know some folks here who can take us around and show us everything that's worth seeing," he said, "and we can spend our time to better advantage here than anywhere else I know of." And sure enough, Bill did know some people in the capital city, some pleasant English people, who had met the open-hearted Westerner when he was in the city years before, and who had at once appreciated the true nobility of his character. They were very kind to Archie,--so kind that the lad thought he had never before met such pleasant people. And they were thoroughly interested in all his adventures, from the time he left home late in the preceding summer until now. He had to tell them all about his New York adventures, and also about their experiences together in the Philippines, and his new friends showed the greatest interest in all he had to say, and seemed to find it all vastly entertaining. They were anxious, Archie thought, to make him have a very good time in Tokio, to make up for some of his hard experiences, and if this were indeed their object, they succeeded admirably in accomplishing it. Every day was filled with surprises, and every night Archie thought he had enjoyed himself more this day than the day before. They travelled about the city so persistently, on foot and in the quaint jinrikishas, that he felt that he knew almost every part of Tokio, and he witnessed every side of native existence, as well as the life in the foreign quarter. It was all charmingly new and interesting, and, as in Hong Kong, they were both sorry when the day for their sailing came around. And always since Archie has declared that no one can be more kindly hospitable than the English.

The voyage from Yokohama to San Francisco was slow and monotonous, Archie thought, for he was now very impatient to reach the United States, and he had also grown very tired of travel by water. There were some very pleasant passengers, but Archie couldn't see that he had a much better time than when he was peeling potatoes corning over. That was interesting enough, anyhow. The only break in the monotony was the day they were enabled to spend in Honolulu, and on that day Archie went again to some of the places he had seen during his first visit to the attractive city. And he called again upon some of the friends of his first visit, and found that most of them had read of his great success as a war correspondent, and of his many exciting experiences in the Philippines. They were all profuse in congratulating him upon what he had accomplished, and every one seemed to think he had been very successful indeed.

While they were in Honolulu a vessel arrived, bound for Japan, and Archie was delighted to find it was the same vessel upon which he had worked his passage from San Francisco on his way to Manila. He went aboard and met some of the friends he had made there, and found that they all knew now who it was they had carried as chore-boy in the galley. They all seemed glad to hear of his success, and to know that he was coming home as a first-class passenger. The cook treated him with much deference, and started to apologise for his treatment of Archie on the way over; but the boy stopped him, and told him that no apology was necessary. "I think I may have been an unwilling worker," he said, "because of course I didn't like the work at all, and it was hard for me to take an interest in peeling potatoes when I was looking forward to accomplishing such great things in the Philippines."

"Oh," said the cook, "you was a fine worker. Sure, I ain't had so good a boy since." And Archie laughed to see the change in opinion which is sometimes brought about by a change in circumstances.

Archie enjoyed the city quite as much as before, but he was glad, nevertheless, when the steamer continued her voyage east. And then he began to count the days until they should arrive in San Francisco, and of course these last days seemed the longest ones of the voyage. But they gradually passed away, and as they steamed ahead, coming nearer every hour to that dear land called "home," both Archie and Bill began to wonder how they would like it all, after their adventurous life in the Philippines. Bill, in particular, was doubtful whether he would again be able to settle down to a quiet existence in some small place, and Archie assured him that he must live in New York, where he would be sure to find things lively enough to suit him.

At last came the eventful day when the great steamer threaded her way through the beautiful Golden Gate, and discharged her passengers at the pier. As Archie and Bill had but little baggage, they were almost the first ones to leave the vessel, and were hurrying away to find a hotel where they could remain overnight when Archie felt some one touch him on the shoulder, and, turning about and seeing no one he knew, was about to go on, when a man introduced himself as being the San Francisco correspondent of the Enterprise. "And these gentlemen here," said he, "are reporters from the newspapers here. They would be glad to have you say a few words about your experiences during the last few months." Archie was quite dumbfounded. It had never occurred to him that he was a person so important as to be interviewed, but he was willing and glad to accommodate the reporters, and told them to accompany him to his hotel. Once there, he answered all their questions, and didn't find it hard at all to give them his opinion of the situation in the Philippines, and what he thought should be done by the government to stop the rebellion. "The President will soon put an end to it," he said, "if he can only have the support of Congress. But as long as there are members of Congress fighting his policy, the insurgents are going to continue their insane efforts to establish an independent government." And some of the reporters smiled to hear so young a fellow talking about the policy in the Philippines. They felt that he was well-informed, however, and put down every word he said.

The interviews over, Archie and Bill went early to bed. The Enterprise correspondent had telegraphed the news of their arrival to New York, and had received word from Mr. Van Bunting to send them on to New York at once. So, early in the morning, the two started for the East, and the train seemed to travel quite as slowly as the steamer. "It does seem good to be in our own country again," they said a hundred times during the days that followed, and when they reached the Empire State and began their journey down the Hudson River, Archie could hardly restrain his enthusiasm at being again in his native commonwealth.

There was quite a delegation at the Grand Central Station to meet them. Mr. Jennings was there in person, and he explained that Mr. Van Bunting was waiting anxiously at the office to see him. Then there were reporters from the various other city papers, who wanted interviews, but Archie was told to say whatever he had to say in the columns of the Enterprise, so he had to deny the reporters for the first time. Bill Hickson was introduced at once, and became the lion of the hour. Every one had read of him, and was glad to shake his hand, and poor Bill was quite bewildered by so much attention. They didn't linger long at the station, however, but hurried down to the Enterprise office, where Mr. Van Bunting was awaiting them. He grasped Archie's hand in his as they entered, and cried, "Well done, my boy, well done." And Archie felt as if he had grown three feet that instant.

CHAPTER XXIV.

DOING "SPECIAL" WORK UPON THE EVENING PAPER--IN-
TERVIEWS WITH FAMOUS MEN--CALLS UPON OLD FRIENDS.

THERE was so much to tell Mr. Jennings and Mr. Van Bunting, that Archie didn't get away from the Enterprise office until seven o'clock in the evening. And what a lot they did say to each other during the afternoon! Archie told of all his experiences, and found them all anxious to hear about them. He learned, to his joy, that everything he had sent had been printed, and that the articles had made a great hit with the public. "We would have liked to keep you there longer, but we knew you must be worn out, and then we want you to stay right here, now, and see if you cannot get us some good interviews and articles of various kinds for the Evening Enterprise. The paper has been losing ground somewhat, of late, and we need some new life for its pages. Of course the morning paper profited greatly by your articles, but the evening edition seemed very weak in comparison, and we think it only fair to Mr. Jennings to let him have you on his staff for awhile now. So if you are willing, you can start in to-morrow as a member of the staff. We will see that you are well paid for what you write, or we will put you on salary, whichever you like. You can think it over, and in the morning you can tell us which plan you like best."

Archie wanted to ask for a few days' absence to return home, but he felt, somehow, that he ought not to ask it just now. So he contented himself with writing a long letter to his mother, in which he enclosed a very large check, money which he had not used on his return to New York. He told her that he would be home just as soon as he could get off for any length of time, and he knew that she would now be looking forward to the visit every day. She had written him about the enthusiasm displayed by every one over his achievements, and how proud she was of what he had accomplished. "I think I am the proudest mother in the country," she wrote one day, and this sentence made Archie very happy, of course, and more anxious than ever to return home. He received a letter, too, from Jack Sullivan, telling him how much the boys all thought of his success, and how every member of the Hut Club had longed time and again to be with him. "It all reads just like some book," Jack wrote, "and we are dying to have you come home and tell us all about it." Then his mother sent him clippings from the town papers, eulogising his efforts, and calling him the "coming man of the State." All this was very pleasant and very encouraging, and Archie couldn't help having a kindly feeling for the townsfolk who thought so much of him.

New York was as delightful as ever. It was now the last of April, and the trees were all green with fresh leaves, and the numerous little parks scattered over the city were looking their very best. The asphalt pavements looked clean and elegant when Archie thought of some other streets he had seen, and the tall office buildings lifted their ornate domes and cupolas into a sky of clear blue. "Surely," he thought to himself, "this is the most charming city in all the world." Fifth Avenue, with its crowds of fashionable folk, and its throng of vehicles, was a delight of which he never tired, and when he went into the Bowery, just to see how things were looking now, he found it quite as interesting and as dirty as in the fall.

But the first place he visited was the dear little square away down-town, where he had lived during those few happy days spent in New York. It, too, looked the same, only the flowers and grass were fresher now, and the fountain seemed to flow more joyously, now that spring was here. The house where he had lodged was as clean as ever, and Archie at once decided to engage a room here, where he could have his New York home. So he called upon the motherly landlady, and was glad to learn that the room he had first was still vacant, and that he could take possession at once.

As before, when he came to this house, Archie was almost out of clothing, so he went out and fitted himself with everything he needed. And this time he felt able to buy the best to be had, for he thought he had now earned the privilege to dress well if he liked. And then, when he had everything he needed to wear, he went out and bought many pretty things for his room, for he felt that he would like to have it just as cosy and home-like as possible. He wasn't able to do much at it this first night, but in the succeeding days he furnished the place in a charming way, so that the landlady said it was the "handsomest room in the house, sir." The dear old lady could hardly understand this great change in her lodger's circumstances. She worried about it very often, and discussed the question with many of the neighbours. "He come here last fall looking mighty poor-like, but, lawsy me, he's as fine now as any man on the avenue." And she never did understand it until one day she learned that her lodger was the "very young man who had been to the war in the Philippines, and writ about his battles in the Enterprise."

There was no ceremony when Archie began work on the evening paper. Mr. Jennings told him that he thought they understood each other pretty well, and that he could use his own discretion, very often, about getting articles. "You can be as independent as you like, Archie," he said, "and use your own ideas as much as you like." This pleased the boy very much indeed. He was beginning to feel now that he had really won his spurs, and that he was a full-fledged journalist. It seemed scarcely possible that it had taken him little more than six months to make this great advance in circumstances, and yet he could see himself a few months previous, sleeping in the station-house. Now his days of poverty were surely over, and he would have a clear path ahead of him to accomplish his great ambition to be a successful author and writer of books. For the present, it was good experience for him to be working upon the Enterprise, and he felt that he ought to be very much contented, since there were men old enough to be his father who were not earning as much money.

He liked the work upon the evening paper very much. He didn't have to get down early in the morning, and at three o'clock in the afternoon he was always through. He was very glad indeed that there was no night work, for he now spent his evenings in studying shorthand, which he thought might be helpful to him in many ways. He didn't have much routine work to do upon the paper in the beginning, but he told Mr. Jennings that he would like to get as much experience as possible, so the good editor gave him a lot of regular reporting to do, as well as the special work which was daily featured in the paper. This special work consisted of interviews with various successful men. Archie had always felt a great admiration for men who had "done something," and as New York was simply filled with wealthy and successful men, who had started as poor boys, he found a wide field for work. He found it very interesting to meet these men of affairs, and have them tell him of their early struggles, how they had begun on the farm or in the factory, and had worked themselves up through industry and perseverance to the high places they now occupied. He found it very easy to get access to most of them, for they had all read of his experiences in the Enterprise, and Archie found that his fame as the "Boy Reporter" was quite general and widespread. Some of the great men were quite as much determined to interview him as he was anxious to interview them, so that he usually got along very well by telling them first of his own experiences, and then asking them about their own boyhood days. It was work that never became monotonous, for each day he saw a man quite different in most respects from the man he had interviewed the day before, and of course every one had something different to say.

These interviews proved very successful when published in the Evening Enterprise, and Mr. Jennings had him continue them during all the weeks Archie was connected with the paper. And of course he did other things, too, work which took him into every part of the great city, looking up this event, or investigating this reported disappearance or murder. Archie was quite successful in this line, too, and, as he was being paid by the column, his weekly income was something larger than he had ever dared to hope for in all his life. He was now enabled to study his stenography at the best school, and to indulge himself in many things which had been denied him before. He could, for instance, attend the performances of grand opera, and hear the great musical artists of the world. He was able, too, to read the best literature, and he gradually learned to appreciate all the many good things in life. He was very glad to find himself broadening in such a way, for he realised that he would not always want to be a "Boy Reporter," and that he had better be developing his mind in every possible way.

He had not been back long in New York before he met all his old friends. One of the first upon whom he called was the good policeman who had been so very kind to him when he had no place to sleep. The large-hearted man was as enthusiastic over his success as if he had been his own son, and Archie felt that here was one true friend upon whom he could always depend. The policeman never tired of telling about that first night when he found Archie walking up and down Broadway, and he always spoke of him to the other officers as "that boy of mine." So the boy, who was now a full-fledged reporter, spent as much time with this friend as possible, and many a time he sat at the station-house telling them all of his adventures in the Orient.

Another friend whom he met was the great railway president with whom he had travelled to Chicago on his way to San Francisco. Archie had liked this man from the very first, and he felt that in him he would always find a friend, because he had shown such interest in his first undertaking. And when he called upon him in his elegant office, he received a very cordial greeting.

"No, indeed," said the great man of affairs, "I have never forgotten our trip West together, and I have followed you with much interest through the columns of the Enterprise. And I am glad that you are back again in New York, for I hope to see a great deal of you. You must come up to my house some evening and tell us all about yourself."

Archie was naturally much surprised to receive an invitation of this kind, but he resolved to accept it, nevertheless.

Bill Hickson was now employed in the Brooklyn navy yard. He had been featured for several days in the Enterprise, and had enjoyed the excitement of New York for awhile, but he decided he would like to be at work. So one day Archie learned that he was working at the navy yard.

"I've got to be with Uncle Sam," was all the reason Bill would give for his action.

CHAPTER XXV.

PRIVATE SECRETARY TO A MILLIONAIRE--STUDYING AT
EVENING SCHOOL--LIVING AMID ELEGANT SURROUNDINGS.

IT was now September. Archie had been in New York the whole summer through, attending carefully to his work on the Evening Enterprise, and continuing his study of stenography. He had taken occasional trips to Long Branch and Asbury Park on Saturday afternoons, but every other day he spent in working up ideas for the paper, and each evening he devoted to the shorthand school. By this time, though, he felt that he knew all that was necessary of shorthand, and found himself more free to go about in the evenings. He visited his friends more frequently, and sometimes spent whole evenings in studying works on English literature, for he was ambitious to know more of the great work he had decided to make his own. This study was not really work to him, for his interest in everything connected with literature was so great that he found a pleasure in reading even the most classical books on the subject, and of course so much reading of this sort did a great deal to educate his mind along this line of work.

One evening in the early fall, Archie decided to accept the invitation of Mr. Depaw, the railway president, to call. So he carefully dressed himself in the best he had, and walked up Fifth Avenue and into the side street where the great man had his home. He rang the bell and presented his card, and waited in the drawing-room for an answer. The footman was gone but a moment, and returning, announced that the family would be down directly. Archie was very much pleased that he was to meet the entire family, and looked about him with great interest at the elegant furnishings of the room in which he sat. He couldn't help thinking how lovely it must be to have so many books, so many pictures, and so many works of art of every kind. The boy thought then that he would like to be a wealthy man, just to be able to gratify his desires for beautiful things.

He had to wait only a short time before the genial Mr. Depaw entered the room, accompanied by several members of the family. Archie was greeted very warmly, and introduced to every one, and then they immediately began an animated conversation, in which Archie soon found himself taking an active part, much to his surprise. He felt that he had never before realised what a great gift it is to be able to talk entertainingly, and this evening was a revelation to him in the ways of good society. He found that every one was much interested in the story of his adventures, and he talked more about them than for a long time past. He was now beginning to feel that his Philippine experiences were an old story, but he learned that they were quite as entertaining as ever to these people. But they did not talk entirely about Archie. They realised that this would be embarrassing to him, and they were careful to guide the conversation into a discussion of music and literature, and whatever else they imagined him to like. And so it was that the evening passed very quickly, and it was time to leave before he knew it. Then he was asked to be sure to call again, and Mr. Depaw, as he accompanied him to the door, requested him to call at his office on the following Wednesday, if possible. Archie promised, and walked home down the avenue, wondering what it could be that Mr. Depaw wanted to talk to him about. He didn't worry long about it, however, but went home and to bed as quickly as possible, for he had formed a habit of rising at six o'clock in the morning to study.

The days passed quickly until Wednesday, and the afternoon of that day found Archie in the waiting-room of Mr. Depaw's office. He had not long to sit there after sending in his card, for the busy man received him as soon as he could get rid of his present visitor. He shook Archie warmly by the hand as he entered, and then, pulling two chairs together, they sat down. "I have been thinking for some time," said Mr. Depaw, "that I need a sort of private secretary. Of course I have men here at the office who take dictation from me, and who fulfil the duties of a secretary to a certain extent, but I want a young man who can attend somewhat to my personal affairs; I want one whom I can trust, and one who is likely to grow as he works along, so that eventually he may be able to fill any place I may have open for him." Then he stopped a moment, and Archie felt his heart beating very fast beneath his coat. He waited almost breathlessly to hear what Mr. Depaw would say next.

"Ever since I met you first," he at last went on, "I have somehow thought that you are the kind of a young fellow I would like. You are ambitious, you are persevering, and you are willing to learn. You say, too, that you know shorthand, and I know that you are a good penman. You have seen quite a little of the world, I am sure, and I think you can prove yourself equal to almost any occasion. The only question is whether you will care to give up reporting for a position of this kind. I can assure you that I will pay you as much as you are earning now, and I shall be glad to offer you a home at my house, because I shall want you at my right hand all the time. Do you think you will care to take the place?"

Archie could hardly speak, it was all so wonderful, but finally he recovered himself sufficiently to explain his hesitancy in accepting the position. "I would like just one day," he said, "to consult with my friends on the newspaper. You see Mr. Jennings and Mr. Van Bunting have been very good to me, and I shouldn't care to leave them now if they object very strongly."

"That's quite right, quite right," said Mr. Depaw. "I can appreciate your feelings, and you can tell the editor that you will have some time for writing, and that you will contribute occasional articles to his paper." Archie was now delighted. "Oh, thank you," he cried. "I am sure I can come now."

"Well, come in at this time to-morrow," said Mr. Depaw, "and let me know what you have decided to do."

Archie hurried at once to Mr. Jennings's office to tell him the good news. He wondered how his friend would take it, but all his fears were soon put at rest. "Archie," said Mr. Jennings, "this is the best opportunity you can ever have to improve yourself in every way. Mr. Depaw is a man highly respected all over the country, and a man who is known to be extraordinary in many ways. Association with such a man will do more for you than four years in college, and you will make a mistake if you do not accept his offer. Of course we shall all be sorry to lose you here, but, as Mr. Depaw says, you will have some time for writing, and we hope you will always continue to do some work for us."

Archie could almost have thrown his arms about Mr. Jennings's neck to hug him for his splendid feeling, and when, a little later, Mr. Van Bunting said practically the same thing, he felt that he had never known two such men. He assured them both that he would never forget them, but would try and spend as much time as possible in the Enterprise office.

The next day he called again on Mr. Depaw, and told him of his decision to accept the place, and the good man seemed overjoyed. "I will see that you never forget it, Archie," he said. It was arranged for him to begin work the very next day. "You can transfer your things to my house as soon as you like, for your room is waiting for you, and I will begin to-morrow to teach you how to do things."

And now Archie found it hard to leave the dear little room in the quaint old square, which was looking now just as when he saw it first. The leaves in the trees were turning brown and gold, and Archie realised that he had been away from home more than a year. "Oh, I must go back soon," he said to himself, "or I shall simply die of homesickness."

In a couple of days he was installed as a member of the Depaw household, and he soon felt at home there. Every one was very kind to him, he was given a handsome room, and everything seemed almost perfect. One of the best things about it all was that he had access to the fine library, and he longed for the long winter evenings when he could devour the many interesting books he saw there. He was soon initiated into his work, and it was much easier than he had expected. Mr. Depaw, of course, started him very gradually, so that he learned as he went along. Every morning at eight o'clock he was in the library with Mr. Depaw, taking dictation, and receiving instructions for the day. They remained together here until ten o'clock, when Mr. Depaw either walked or drove to his office. Archie always accompanied him, and took charge of some of the mail there, attending to it during the morning. Then at noon he returned to the house, where he spent the afternoon in writing the letters which had been dictated in the morning, and in doing various things for Mr. Depaw. The evenings he always had to himself, and he had no difficulty in finding enough to do at home without going out. He almost invariably passed the evenings in reading, but occasionally he was asked to accompany the family to some musical event at the opera house, for they had soon learned of his love for music.

In work and study the winter passed quickly and happily for Archie, who now felt quite at ease amid his elegant surroundings. His only wish was that he might go home, and as spring approached Mr. Depaw promised him that he should have a short vacation. The suggestion of Mr. Depaw that Archie's mother come to New

York for a week was heartily accepted by Archie, but when he wrote home Mrs. Dunn replied that she would rather wait for Archie at home. She had never visited New York, and felt that she wouldn't like it.

Bill Hickson came over very often from the navy yard, and was always a welcome visitor at Mr. Depaw's office. He didn't seem to care for his work in Brooklyn, however, and Archie finally requested a place for him about the elegant new station which the road had just constructed in the city. Mr. Depaw very readily gave him an excellent position, one which he could keep always if he so desired. And Bill was highly pleased with his new work, so much so that he surprised them all one day in the spring by leading into the once a young lady whom he introduced as his wife. Of course Archie was very much pleased at this new development, for he had often thought that his friend must be very lonely, living in a boarding-house.

The days were all busy ones for Archie now. He had learned the work so thoroughly that he was given more than ever to do, and he still continued to write, too, for the Enterprise. He worked too hard, however, and in April he looked so thin that Mr. Depaw sent him home for a week's rest.

CHAPTER XXVI.

DECIDES TO VISIT HOME--A GREAT RECEPTION IN THE TOWN--A PUBLIC   CHARACTER NOW--DINNER TO THE HUT CLUB--DEMONSTRATION AT THE TOWN HALL-- A   TELEGRAM FROM HIS EMPLOYER LEAVING FOR EUROPE.

IT was a beautiful April day. There had been a light shower in the morning, and now everything looked as fresh and green as possible all along the railway. Archie lay back in his comfortable Wagner seat, admiring the beauties of spring, and thinking, too, of the days he spent in walking along this very road. It seemed hard to believe that he was now secretary to the president of this railroad, and that he was returning home, after a year and a half, a very successful young man. He had much to think of in the hours it would take him to reach the little town. He tried to remember everything about the place, and his mother as he saw her last, and it wasn't at all difficult for him to do so. But, oh, how he hoped that things had not changed! He almost dreaded going home for fear he would find things different.

He had changed, that much was sure. He knew that he had grown to look much older than his years, and he knew that he was not looking particularly strong. He used to be so sturdy, and he had such a splendid colour in his cheeks. Mother would be sorry to see him now, but of course he would be sure to improve very much during the week he was to remain among old friends.

He was very anxious to see his boy friends, the members of the Hut Club, and the boys and girls who were in his class at school. He had telegraphed his mother that he was coming, so she would probably tell the boys about it. He was sure they would be there.

Now the stations looked more familiar. This one just passed was near the Tinch farm, and Archie remembered the days he spent working for old Hiram, and how he had suffered. He wondered if the farmer had ever seen any copies of the Enterprise. It would be very interesting to him to know that his chore-boy was now a secretary to a millionaire. This next station he remembered very well indeed, because he used to come here every fall to visit the county fair, where he marvelled at the wonderful things he saw in the side-shows.

And now the train was entering the limits of his own town. Here was the old elevator, and the machine shop near the railway track. And, oh, there was his own home, looking green and pleasant as the train sped by. It almost brought tears to Archie's eyes to think that he was so soon to see his mother. Now they had reached the station, and he stood upon the car platform ready to alight. My, what a crowd there was! and why did they cheer as he made his appearance? All at once it dawned upon him that all these people were here to meet him, and to bid him welcome home. He could hardly speak as he found himself in his mother's arms, and then he began to shake the hands of the big crowd. They were all old friends, and then there was the mayor, and the superintendent of schools, and quite a delegation of leading citizens. How nice it was of them to welcome him in this way!

After awhile the handshaking was over, and the mayor was able to get a few minutes with Archie. "We are all very proud of what you have accomplished," he said, "and we want to give you a public reception to-morrow night in the town hall, if you don't object." Archie stared blankly at the mayor, and it was several moments before he realised the meaning of the words. Then he was almost overcome. It was almost too good to be true, it seemed, but he warmly thanked the mayor, and told him how he appreciated the honour which they had done him. He said that he would be glad to attend the reception.

The crowd was scattering now, and Archie, wild to reach home, took his mother to a carriage, in which they drove rapidly out to the little house among the trees and arbours. The old town looked beautiful in every way. The great maple and oak trees along the road were green with new leaves, and every dooryard was bright with snowballs and yellow roses. "This is the very best time of the year," he said to his mother, "and I am the very happiest boy in all the world."

"And I am the happiest mother," was the answer. Then they sat in silence until they reached the old home. They entered by the kitchen door, and, once inside, and seated in the old cane rocking-chair, Archie bowed his head in tears of joy at being home with mother once again.

The hours which followed were sweet with joy. Mrs. Dunn busied herself in preparing the supper, and Archie hung around the kitchen, telling some of the many things he had planned to tell. Mrs. Dunn was smiling, and Archie thought her the sweetest mother any boy could have. She was changed somewhat, but she looked very young to-day.

Supper over, Archie went over the fence to see the Sullivan boys, and he found them looking much the same. He was truly glad to see them, and they, of course, were glad to see him, too, though at first they were just a little bashful, remembering, no doubt, all the things which had happened to Archie since they saw him last. The boys were soon telling all about the Hut Club, though, and Archie learned to his joy that it was still a flourishing organisation. "We spoke of you every time we were together," said Jack, "and we always wished you were back again." Archie was delighted to hear that he had been missed, and all at once an idea came to him which he put into execution three days later. He determined to give an elegant dinner to this club of boys, and the very next day he sent to New York for a caterer to arrange it. He wanted it to be something finer than any of the boys had ever seen, and it certainly turned out to be so. The caterer did his best, and when, three days later, the Hut Club sat down together for the first time in more than eighteen months, they partook of a dinner which would have done credit to Mr. Depaw's table. It was a memorable night for them all, and every boy enjoyed himself.

Archie enjoyed this Hut Club dinner more than anything else while he was at home, though of course the great event of his stay was the public reception at the Town Hall on the second evening after his arrival. This was a truly grand affair. The town authorities hired a brass band, which played inside the hall and out, and there was such a crowd in attendance that many were turned away from the doors. It was a night that Archie will never be able to forget. He sat on the platform, in company with the mayor and other town officials, and he listened to several speeches congratulating him on what he had accomplished since leaving the town. Then he had to get up and tell them all of his experiences, from the time he left until now. He told it in a simple manner, but from the close attention he received it was evident his audience was deeply interested. When he had finished, there were calls for "three cheers for Archie Dunn," and they were given with a will. Then Archie, rising from his seat, called for "three cheers for the President of the United States," and they, too, were given, for Archie had told them all his feelings on the subject of the President's policy in the war. After this there were three cheers for Mr. Depaw, whom one man said would be the next United States Senator from the State. The meeting closed with some cheers for the New York Enterprise, and then followed a long siege of handshaking for Archie, who stood beside his mother on the floor in front of the platform. It was a happy night for them both, and Mrs. Dunn said afterward that she could never wish for anything more the rest of her life.

The fourth day of his visit was a Sunday, and, to Archie's joy, brave Bill Hickson and his wife came up from the city to spend the day. What a jolly time they had, all day long! They went to church in the morning, where they saw all the people, it seemed, whom they hadn't seen before, and in the afternoon there were many callers at the little house. The evening was spent quietly by the happy four, talking of old times and plans for the future. The town authorities were anxious to give Bill Hickson a reception while he was in town, but the bashful hero declined the honour, and returned with his wife to New York by the midnight train.

During the two succeeding days Archie talked a great deal with his mother, and finally gained her consent to come to New York to live in a year's time. Mrs. Dunn had never really understood that Archie had so good a position, but now that she realised what a splendid beginning he had made, she was very willing to come and keep house for him. This question settled, everything seemed wholly delightful in the cosy home, and Archie settled down to enjoy the two remaining days of his visit in quiet rest. He had already much improved during his stay, and was sure of going back to the city feeling much better than for a long time past, and this made Mrs. Dunn very happy.

But Archie didn't stay his week out at home. On the fifth night he attended a reception in his honour at one of the neighbours' houses, and he was just in the midst of a description of Tokio when a messenger boy entered with a telegram for him. He opened it at once, and read it aloud to the company:

"Dear Archie," it said, "return as soon as possible. I sail for Europe on Saturday's steamer to remain six months, and wish you to accompany me." It was signed by

Mr. Depaw, and there was great applause from the crowd when he finished reading it. But Archie's face was a study. He wasn't sure whether he wanted to go to Europe or not, but of course there was no question about what he should do. He at once telegraphed a reply, saying that he would reach the city to-morrow at noon, leaving home on the early morning train.

Of course the reception soon broke up, and Archie walked quietly home with his mother, who was saddened at the prospect of losing him so soon again. She soon brightened, however, and began to plan things for him to do abroad, and soon she entered into the preparation for his departure with all her heart. But Archie was not so soon made glad, and he didn't rest until he made his mother promise to accompany him to the city on the morrow to spend the two days previous to his departure in helping him get ready. Mrs. Dunn wasn't anxious to make the trip, but for Archie's sake she consented.

And early the next morning they left for the city, where the time passed rapidly until the hour of the steamer's sailing. At the pier they said good-bye. Archie could hardly speak, but Mrs. Dunn was brave. "Archie," she said, "God has been with you so far and he will keep you yet. And remember that a boy with honest ambition will always get along. You are sure to have friends about you always, for you have proved that you possess energy, perseverance and a good heart." She said good-bye without a tear, but as the steamer left the pier Archie saw, on looking back, a sweet mother seated on a coil of rope, with her handkerchief to her eyes.

THE END.

The Codes Of Hammurabi And Moses
W. W. Davies

QTY

The discovery of the Hammurabi Code is one of the greatest achievements of archaeology, and is of paramount interest, not only to the student of the Bible, but also to all those interested in ancient history...

Religion   **ISBN:** *1-59462-338-4*   **Pages:132**
MSRP $12.95

The Theory of Moral Sentiments
Adam Smith

QTY

This work from 1749. contains original theories of conscience amd moral judgment and it is the foundation for systemof morals.

Philosophy   **ISBN:** *1-59462-777-0*   **Pages:536**
MSRP $19.95

Jessica's First Prayer
Hesba Stretton

QTY

In a screened and secluded corner of one of the many railway-bridges which span the streets of London there could be seen a few years ago, from five o'clock every morning until half past eight, a tidily set-out coffee-stall, consisting of a trestle and board, upon which stood two large tin cans, with a small fire of charcoal burning under each so as to keep the coffee boiling during the early hours of the morning when the work-people were thronging into the city on their way to their daily toil...

Pages:84

Childrens   **ISBN:** *1-59462-373-2*   *MSRP $9.95*

My Life and Work
Henry Ford

QTY

Henry Ford revolutionized the world with his implementation of mass production for the Model T automobile. Gain valuable business insight into his life and work with his own auto-biography... "We have only started on our development of our country we have not as yet, with all our talk of wonderful progress, done more than scratch the surface. The progress has been wonderful enough but..."

Pages:300

Biographies/   **ISBN:** *1-59462-198-5*   *MSRP $21.95*

The Art of Cross-Examination
Francis Wellman

QTY

I presume it is the experience of every author, after his first book is published upon an important subject, to be almost overwhelmed with a wealth of ideas and illustrations which could readily have been included in his book, and which to his own mind, at least, seem to make a second edition inevitable. Such certainly was the case with me; and when the first edition had reached its sixth impression in five months, I rejoiced to learn that it seemed to my publishers that the book had met with a sufficiently favorable reception to justify a second and considerably enlarged edition. ...

Reference   ISBN: *1-59462-647-2*

Pages:412

MSRP $19.95

On the Duty of Civil Disobedience
Henry David Thoreau

QTY

Thoreau wrote his famous essay, On the Duty of Civil Disobedience, as a protest against an unjust but popular war and the immoral but popular institution of slave-owning. He did more than write—he declined to pay his taxes, and was hauled off to gaol in consequence. Who can say how much this refusal of his hastened the end of the war and of slavery ?

Law   ISBN: *1-59462-747-9*

Pages:48

MSRP $7.45

Dream Psychology Psychoanalysis for Beginners
Sigmund Freud

QTY

Sigmund Freud, born Sigismund Schlomo Freud (May 6, 1856 - September 23, 1939), was a Jewish-Austrian neurologist and psychiatrist who co-founded the psychoanalytic school of psychology. Freud is best known for his theories of the unconscious mind, especially involving the mechanism of repression; his redefinition of sexual desire as mobile and directed towards a wide variety of objects; and his therapeutic techniques, especially his understanding of transference in the therapeutic relationship and the presumed value of dreams as sources of insight into unconscious desires.

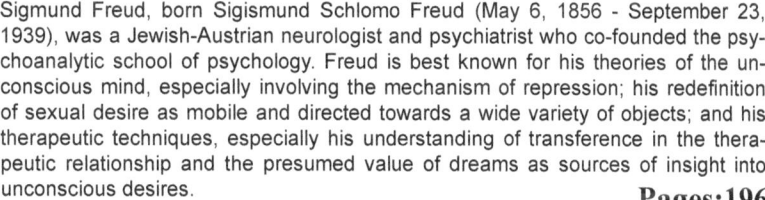

Psychology   ISBN: *1-59462-905-6*

Pages:196

MSRP $15.45

The Miracle of Right Thought
Orison Swett Marden

QTY

Believe with all of your heart that you will do what you were made to do. When the mind has once formed the habit of holding cheerful, happy, prosperous pictures, it will not be easy to form the opposite habit. It does not matter how improbable or how far away this realization may see, or how dark the prospects may be, if we visualize them as best we can, as vividly as possible, hold tenaciously to them and vigorously struggle to attain them, they will gradually become actualized, realized in the life. But a desire, a longing without endeavor, a yearning abandoned or held indifferently will vanish without realization.

Pages:360

Self Help   ISBN: *1-59462-644-8*

MSRP $25.45

QTY

The Rosicrucian Cosmo-Conception Mystic Christianity *by Max Heindel*   ISBN: *1-59462-188-8* **$38.95**
The Rosicrucian Cosmo-conception is not dogmatic, neither does it appeal to any other authority than the reason of the student. It is: not controversial, but is: sent forth in the, hope that it may help to clear...   New Age/Religion Pages 646

Abandonment To Divine Providence *by Jean-Pierre de Caussade*   ISBN: *1-59462-228-0* **$25.95**
"The Rev. Jean Pierre de Caussade was one of the most remarkable spiritual writers of the Society of Jesus in France in the 18th Century. His death took place at Toulouse in 1751. His works have gone through many editions and have been republished...   Inspirational/Religion Pages 400

Mental Chemistry *by Charles Haanel*   ISBN: *1-59462-192-6* **$23.95**
Mental Chemistry allows the change of material conditions by combining and appropriately utilizing the power of the mind. Much like applied chemistry creates something new and unique out of careful combinations of chemicals the mastery of mental chemistry...   New Age Pages 354

The Letters of Robert Browning and Elizabeth Barret Barrett 1845-1846 vol II   ISBN: *1-59462-193-4* **$35.95**
by Robert Browning and Elizabeth Barrett   Biographies Pages 596

Gleanings In Genesis (volume I) *by Arthur W. Pink*   ISBN: *1-59462-130-6* **$27.45**
Appropriately has Genesis been termed "the seed plot of the Bible" for in it we have, in germ form, almost all of the great doctrines which are afterwards fully developed in the books of Scripture which follow...   Religion/Inspirational Pages 420

The Master Key *by L. W. de Laurence*   ISBN: *1-59462-001-6* **$30.95**
In no branch of human knowledge has there been a more lively increase of the spirit of research during the past few years than in the study of Psychology, Concentration and Mental Discipline. The requests for authentic lessons in Thought Control, Mental Discipline and...   New Age/Business Pages 422

The Lesser Key Of Solomon Goetia *by L. W. de Laurence*   ISBN: *1-59462-092-X* **$9.95**
This translation of the first book of the "Lernegton" which is now for the first time made accessible to students of Talismanic Magic was done, after careful collation and edition, from numerous Ancient Manuscripts in Hebrew, Latin, and French...   New Age/Occult Pages 92

Rubaiyat Of Omar Khayyam *by Edward Fitzgerald*   ISBN:*1-59462-332-5* **$13.95**
Edward Fitzgerald, whom the world has already learned, in spite of his own efforts to remain within the shadow of anonymity, to look upon as one of the rarest poets of the century, was born at Bredfield, in Suffolk, on the 31st of March, 1809. He was the third son of John Purcell...   Music Pages 172

Ancient Law *by Henry Maine*   ISBN: *1-59462-128-4* **$29.95**
The chief object of the following pages is to indicate some of the earliest ideas of mankind, as they are reflected in Ancient Law, and to point out the relation of those ideas to modern thought.   Religion/History Pages 452

Far-Away Stories *by William J. Locke*   ISBN: *1-59462-129-2* **$19.45**
"Good wine needs no bush, but a collection of mixed vintages does. And this book is just such a collection. Some of the stories I do not want to remain buried for ever in the museum files of dead magazine-numbers an author's not unpardonable vanity..."   Fiction Pages 272

Life of David Crockett *by David Crockett*   ISBN: *1-59462-250-7* **$27.45**
"Colonel David Crockett was one of the most remarkable men of the times in which he lived. Born in humble life, but gifted with a strong will, an indomitable courage, and unremitting perseverance...   Biographies/New Age Pages 424

Lip-Reading *by Edward Nitchie*   ISBN: *1-59462-206-X* **$25.95**
Edward B. Nitchie, founder of the New York School for the Hard of Hearing, now the Nitchie School of Lip-Reading, Inc, wrote "LIP-READING Principles and Practice". The development and perfecting of this meritorious work on lip-reading was an undertaking...   How-to Pages 400

A Handbook of Suggestive Therapeutics, Applied Hypnotism, Psychic Science   ISBN: *1-59462-214-0* **$24.95**
by Henry Munro   Health/New Age/Health/Self-help Pages 376

A Doll's House: and Two Other Plays *by Henrik Ibsen*   ISBN: *1-59462-112-8* **$19.95**
Henrik Ibsen created this classic when in revolutionary 1848 Rome. Introducing some striking concepts in playwriting for the realist genre, this play has been studied the world over.   Fiction/Classics/Plays 308

The Light of Asia *by sir Edwin Arnold*   ISBN: *1-59462-204-3* **$13.95**
In this poetic masterpiece, Edwin Arnold describes the life and teachings of Buddha. The man who was to become known as Buddha to the world was born as Prince Gautama of India but he rejected the worldly riches and abandoned the reigns of power when...   Religion/History/Biographies Pages 170

The Complete Works of Guy de Maupassant *by Guy de Maupassant*   ISBN: *1-59462-157-8* **$16.95**
"For days and days, nights and nights, I had dreamed of that first kiss which was to consecrate our engagement, and I knew not on what spot I should put my lips..."   Fiction/Classics Pages 240

The Art of Cross-Examination *by Francis L. Wellman*   ISBN: *1-59462-309-0* **$26.95**
Written by a renowned trial lawyer, Wellman imparts his experience and uses case studies to explain how to use psychology to extract desired information through questioning.   How-to/Science/Reference Pages 408

Answered or Unanswered? *by Louisa Vaughan*   ISBN: *1-59462-248-5* **$10.95**
Miracles of Faith in China   Religion Pages 112

The Edinburgh Lectures on Mental Science (1909) *by Thomas*   ISBN: *1-59462-008-3* **$11.95**
This book contains the substance of a course of lectures recently given by the writer in the Queen Street Hall, Edinburgh. Its purpose is to indicate the Natural Principles governing the relation between Mental Action and Material Conditions...   New Age Psychology Pages 148

Ayesha *by H. Rider Haggard*   ISBN: *1-59462-301-5* **$24.95**
Verily and indeed it is the unexpected that happens! Probably if there was one person upon the earth from whom the Editor of this, and of a certain previous history, did not expect to hear again...   Classics Pages 380

Ayala's Angel *by Anthony Trollope*   ISBN: *1-59462-352-X* **$29.95**
The two girls were both pretty, but Lucy who was twenty-one who supposed to be simple and comparatively unattractive, whereas Ayala was credited, as her Bombwhat romantic name might show, with poetic charm and a taste for romance. Ayala when her father died was nineteen...   Fiction Pages 484

The American Commonwealth *by James Bryce*   ISBN: *1-59462-286-8* **$34.45**
An interpretation of American democratic political theory. It examines political mechanics and society from the perspective of Scotsman James Bryce   Politics Pages 572

Stories of the Pilgrims *by Margaret P. Pumphrey*   ISBN: *1-59462-116-0* **$17.95**
This book explores pilgrims religious oppression in England as well as their escape to Holland and eventual crossing to America on the Mayflower, and their early days in New England...   History Pages 268

QTY

The Fasting Cure *by Sinclair Upton* ISBN: *1-59462-222-1* **$13.95**
In the Cosmopolitan Magazine for May, 1910, and in the Contemporary Review (London) for April, 1910, I published an article dealing with my experiences in fasting. I have written a great many magazine articles, but never one which attracted so much attention... New Age/Self Help/Health Pages 164

Hebrew Astrology *by Sepharial* ISBN: *1-59462-308-2* **$13.45**
In these days of advanced thinking it is a matter of common observation that we have left many of the old landmarks behind and that we are now pressing forward to greater heights and to a wider horizon than that which represented the mind-content of our progenitors... Astrology Pages 144

Thought Vibration or The Law of Attraction in the Thought World ISBN: *1-59462-127-6* **$12.95**
by William Walker Atkinson *Psychology/Religion Pages 144*

Optimism *by Helen Keller* ISBN: *1-59462-108-X* **$15.95**
Helen Keller was blind, deaf, and mute since 19 months old, yet famously learned how to overcome these handicaps, communicate with the world, and spread her lectures promoting optimism. An inspiring read for everyone... Biographies/Inspirational Pages 84

Sara Crewe *by Frances Burnett* ISBN: *1-59462-360-0* **$9.45**
In the first place, Miss Minchin lived in London. Her home was a large, dull, tall one, in a large, dull square, where all the houses were alike, and all the sparrows were alike, and where all the door-knockers made the same heavy sound... Childrens/Classic Pages 88

The Autobiography of Benjamin Franklin *by Benjamin Franklin* ISBN: *1-59462-135-7* **$24.95**
The Autobiography of Benjamin Franklin has probably been more extensively read than any other American historical work, and no other book of its kind has had such ups and downs of fortune. Franklin lived for many years in England, where he was agent... Biographies/History Pages 332

Name	
Email	
Telephone	
Address	
City, State ZIP	

☐ **Credit Card**   ☐ **Check / Money Order**

Credit Card Number	
Expiration Date	
Signature	

Please Mail to: Book Jungle
PO Box 2226
Champaign, IL 61825
or Fax to: 630-214-0564

ORDERING INFORMATION

web: *www.bookjungle.com*
email: *sales@bookjungle.com*
fax: *630-214-0564*
mail: *Book Jungle PO Box 2226 Champaign, IL 61825*
or PayPal *to sales@bookjungle.com*

Please contact us for bulk discounts

DIRECT-ORDER TERMS

**20% Discount if You Order
Two or More Books**
Free Domestic Shipping!
Accepted: Master Card, Visa,
Discover, American Express

www.ingramcontent.com/pod-product-compliance
Lightning Source LLC
Chambersburg PA
CBHW080746250626
47162CB00010B/3036